張文娟 著

中級 Reading & Writing

NEW

新制全民英檢

GEPT

The General English Proficiency Test [Intermediate]

閱讀&寫作 模擬試題 +解答

CONTENTS
目錄

The General English Proficiency Test [Intermediate]

第四章
閱讀模擬試題

CONTENTS
目錄

第五章
寫作模擬試題

第六章
520 個最常考的中級字彙

前言

1. 關於全民英檢 [中級]： 閱讀 & 寫作的 問與答（Q&A）

Q：「全民英語能力分級檢定測驗」的由來？

A：在國際化的趨勢下，推展全民英語學習運動已成為教育界及民間普遍的共識，而語言訓練測驗中心多年來辦理外語能力測驗的經驗也顯示國內需要一套完整並具公信力之英語能力分級檢定系統，以適應各級教育及社會各階層的需求，因此在 86 年度邀集國內相關領域之學者專家成立研究及諮詢委員會，開始著手研發這項測驗系統，希望能夠提供國內各階段英語學習者公平、可靠、具效度的英語能力評量工具。

Q: 這項測驗各級數命題方向為何？考生應如何準備？

A:「全民英檢」各級數的命題方向均參考國內各級英語教育之課程大綱，同時也廣泛蒐集相關教材進行內容分析，以求命題內容能符合國內各級英語教育指標。此外，這項測驗的內容反映本土的生活經驗與特色，因此命題內容生活化，並包含流行話題及時事。

Q: 通過「全民英檢」合格標準者是否取得合格證書？又合格證書有何用途或效力？

A: 是的，語言訓練測驗中心將於寄發複試成績單時一併寄發合格證書給通過「全民英檢」之聽、說、讀、寫四項測驗者。目前「全民英檢」已經為全國公務人員陞任加分、教育部公費留考及大學甄選入學招生採用，並獲中華航空公司、台北捷運公司、台灣金融研訓院等多家公民營機構採認作為人力評估及招募人才之參考，此外，台大、台師大、交大等多所大學及高中亦採用作為學習成果評量或畢業檢核依據。

Q:「全民英檢」中級之檢測程度為何？

A: 中級具有使用簡單英語進行日常生活溝通的能力，相當於高中畢業程度。

Q:「全民英檢」中級閱讀測驗和寫作測驗之分數如何計算？

A: 中級閱讀測驗成績計分方式採標準計分，如以傳統粗分計分概念來說，閱讀測驗每題 3 分，各項得分為答對題數乘以每題分數，可以大概計算是否通過。寫作測驗成績採整體式評分，使用級分制，分為 0~5 級分，再轉換成百分制，達 80 分以上視為通過。

中級 Reading & Writing

NEW

新制全民英檢

GEPT
The General English Proficiency Test [Intermediate]

閱讀&寫作 模擬試題 +解答

Q: 寫作測驗既採非選擇題方式，評分方式為何？

A: 寫作能力測驗採人工閱卷，每位考生的作答均經由受過訓練的合格評分老師評閱，評分係根據「全民英檢」各級數寫作測驗分數說明，經初、複審程序進行。評分期間並有專人持續追蹤評分老師的評分情形，確認每位評分老師均穩定掌握評分指標。

Q: 考後會公布試題及答案嗎？

A:「全民英檢」經諮詢委員會決議，不逐一公布歷次測驗試題。

Q: 可不可以知道自己錯在哪裡？

A: 本測驗為標準參照測驗，無法提供作答錯誤資料分析及錯誤更正說明。

Q: 合格證書有期限嗎？

A: 證書永久有效，惟欲申請加發合格證書或成績單須於測驗日起 2 年內提出（非指證書的效期為 2 年），逾期申請無法受理。

2. 各級能力說明

➡綜合能力說明：

初級（Elementary）

具有基礎英語能力，能理解和使用淺易日常用語。

建議下列人員宜具有該級英語能力：

一般行政助理、維修技術人員、百貨業、餐飲業、旅館業或觀光景點服務人員、計程車駕駛等。

中級（Intermediate）

具有使用簡單英語進行日常生活溝通的能力。

建議下列人員宜具有該級英語能力：

一般行政、業務、技術、銷售人員、護理人員、旅館／飯店接待人員、總機人員、 警政人員、旅遊從業人員等。

中高級（High-Intermediate）

英語能力逐漸成熟，應用的領域擴大，雖有錯誤，但無礙溝通。

建議下列人員宜具有該級英語能力：

商務、企劃人員、祕書、工程師、研究助理、空服人員、航空機師、航管人員、海關人員、導遊、外事警政人員、新聞從業人員、資訊管理人員等。

高級（Advanced）

英語流利順暢，僅有少許錯誤，應用能力擴及學術或專業領域。

建議下列人員宜具有該級英語能力：

高級商務人員、協商談判人員、英語教學人員、研究人員、翻譯人員、外交人員、國際新聞從業人員等。

優級（Superior）

英語能力接近受過高等教育之母語人士，各種場合均能使用適當策略作最有效的溝通。

建議下列人員宜具有該級英語能力：

專業翻譯人員、國際新聞特派人員、外交官員、協商談判主談人員等。

➥各級分項能力說明：

初級

聽：能聽懂與日常生活相關的淺易談話，包括價格、時間及地點等。

讀：可看懂與日常生活相關的淺易英文，並能閱讀路標、交通標誌、招牌、簡單菜單、時刻表及賀卡等。

說：能朗讀簡易文章、簡單地自我介紹，對熟悉的話題能以簡易英語對答，如問候、購物、問路等。

寫：能寫簡單的句子及段落，如寫明信片、便條、賀卡及填表格等。對一般日常生活相關的事物，能以簡短的文字敘述或說明。

中級

聽：在日常生活中，能聽懂一般的會話；能大致聽懂公共場所廣播、氣象報告及廣告等。在工作時，能聽懂簡易的產品介紹與操作說明。能大致聽懂外籍人士的談話及詢問。

讀：在日常生活中，能閱讀短文、故事、私人信件、廣告、傳單、簡介及使用說明等。在工作時，能閱讀工作須知、公告、操作手冊、例行的文件、傳真、電報等。

說：在日常生活中，能以簡易英語交談或描述一般事物，能介紹自己的生活作息、工作、家庭、經歷等，並可對一般話題陳述看法。在工作時，能進行簡單的答詢，並與外籍人士交談溝通。

寫：能寫簡單的書信、故事及心得等。對於熟悉且與個人經歷相關的主題，能以簡易的文字表達。

中高級

聽：在日常生活中，能聽懂社交談話，並能大致聽懂一般的演講、報導及節目等。在工作時，能聽懂簡報、討論、產品介紹及操作說明等。

讀：在日常生活中，能閱讀書信、說明書及報章雜誌等。在工作時，能閱讀一般文件、摘要、會議紀錄及報告等。

說：在日常生活中，對與個人興趣相關的話題，能流暢地表達意見及看法。在工作時，能接待外籍人士、介紹工作內容、洽談業務、在會議中發言，並能做簡報。

寫：能寫一般的工作報告及書信等。除日常生活相關主題外，與工作相關的事物、時事及較複雜或抽象的概念皆能適當表達。

高級

聽：在日常生活中，能聽懂各類主題的談話、辯論、演講、報導及節目等。在工作時，參與業務會議或談判時，能聽懂報告及討論的內容。

讀：能閱讀各類不同主題、體裁的文章，包括報章雜誌、文學作品、專業期刊、學術著作及文獻等。

說：對於各類主題皆能流暢地表達看法、參與討論，能在一般會議或專業研討會中報告或發表意見等。

　　寫：能寫一般及專業性摘要、報告、論文、新聞報導等，可翻譯一般書籍及新聞等。對各類主題均能表達看法，並作深入探討。

優級

　　聽：能聽懂各類主題及體裁的內容，理解程度與受過高等教育之母語人士相當。

　　讀：能閱讀各類不同主題、體裁文章。閱讀速度及理解程度與受過高等教育之母語人士相當。

　　說：能在各種不同場合以正確流利之英語表達看法；能適切引用文化知識及慣用語詞。

　　寫：能撰寫不同性質的文章，如企劃報告、專業／學術性摘要、論文、新聞報導及時事評論等。對於各類主題均能有效完整地闡述並作深入探討。

　　以上摘錄自全民英檢官網

中級 Reading & Writing

NEW

新制全民英檢
GEPT

The General English Proficiency Test [Intermediate]

閱讀&寫作 模擬試題 +解答

CHAPTER

2

閱讀講座

中級 Reading & Writing
新制全民英檢
GEPT
The General English Proficiency Test [Intermediate]

NEW

閱讀&寫作 模擬試題 +解答

1. 平日培養英文閱讀能力 的方法

　　平時就要訓練自己對周圍的英文有強烈的敏銳度，同時要培養良好的閱讀習慣。可以從自己感興趣的英文讀物著手，例如流行時尚網站或電玩動漫雜誌等等，接著朝適合自己程度的短篇文章或簡短故事來努力，搭配著全民英檢題庫的閱讀測驗，檢測自己的學習成果，隨時培養英文閱讀能力，不斷鞭策自己向下一個學習目標前進。

　　以下是一些可以供參考的英文閱讀能力訓練方法：

　　☆多注意周圍的英文，例如報章雜誌或電視廣告等媒體上出現的英文。

　　☆多讀英文短篇故事（中英對照亦可）或英語學習口袋書。

　　☆多閱讀英語學習雜誌。

　　☆多做全民英檢閱讀模擬試題。

　　☆善用網路資源，例如英文網路報紙的學生版。

　　☆邊讀邊記：瀏覽全文後，找出關鍵字並快速做摘要。

2. 如何針對全民英檢中級閱讀作準備

本測驗分三部分,全為四選一之選擇題,共 40 題,作答時間 45 分鐘。

中級 Reading & Writing
新制全民英檢
GEPT
The General English Proficiency Test [Intermediate]
NEW
閱讀&寫作 模擬試題 +解答

第一部分：詞彙和結構

共 15 題，每題含一個空格。請由試題冊上的四個選項中選出最適合題意的字或詞作答。

例：

After the police arrive, they will begin to interview the people who
_____ in the jewelry store at the time of the robbery.

A. have been

B. will be

C. were

D. are

正確答案為 C，請在答案紙上塗黑作答。

☆本部分要測驗的是：一個單字或片語在一個句子中的正確使用方法，也就是基本的文法。

☆準備方法：平時就要不斷儲備單字和片語量，重點是要學會如何在合宜的上下文中靈活運用這些單字和片語，而不是死記。方法不外乎大量閱讀，並且多做全民英檢模擬試題，做完後確實檢討，並且將題目和選項中出現的新單字和新片語也一併學起來，因為這些都是出現頻率極高的單字和片語，在其他題目中很可能也會再出現。

第二部分：段落填空

　　共 10 題，包括二個段落，每個段落各含 5 個空格。請由試題冊上四個選項中選出最適合題意的字或詞作答。

　　例：

Susan had a terrible day today. First she (1) up by a strange phone call at four o'clock this morning. When she was about to (2) the receiver, the phone stopped ringing. Then, she got up late and (3) the company bus, so she was thirty minutes late for work, (4) made her boss very angry. What was (5) , when she got home this afternoon, she couldn't open the door because she had left her keys at her office.

1. A. woke
   B. was woken
   C. wakes
   D. is awake　　（正確答案：B）

2. A. pick up
   B. pick
   C. pick at
   D. pick on　　（正確答案：A）

中級 Reading & Writing

NEW

新制全民英檢

GEPT

The General English Proficiency Test [Intermediate]

閱讀&寫作 模擬試題 +解答

3. A. dropped

   B. lost

   C. missed

   D. left　　　（正確答案：C）

4. A. that

   B. this

   C. what

   D. which　　　（正確答案：D）

5. A. harder

   B. worse

   C. later

   D. angrier　　（正確答案：B）

　　☆本部分要測驗的是：是否能在一個段落或一篇短文中正確使用單字和片語，是否能夠掌握字句和語意的連貫性和完整性，亦即是否懂得一篇英文短文的基本架構和邏輯連貫，也就是英語寫作的基本章法。

　　☆準備方法：除了和準備第一部分一樣要多背單字、片語和多做模擬測驗外，還要多讀作文範例，學習英文佳作中簡潔有條理的表達方式，不斷培養語感，如此一來，這個測驗項目就會變得輕而易舉了。

第三部分：閱讀理解

　　共 15 題，包括數篇短文，每篇短文後有 2~4 個相關問題。請由試題冊上四個選項中選出最適合者作答。

　　☆本部分要測驗的是：在有限的時間內，迅速掌握一篇文章的大旨，並且能快速找到所要搜尋的資訊。

　　☆準備方法：運用略讀（skimming）與掃讀（scanning）的技巧，妥善分配各篇文章中各題所需的時間，從容作答。

　　略讀（skimming）：快速瀏覽全文，以獲得大意。
　　掃讀（scanning）：快速掃描整篇文章，以獲得特定的細節性資訊。

　　先快速瀏覽全文，尤其是文章的開端，因為那經常就是一篇文章的主旨，略讀的技巧是在瀏覽時專注於關鍵字：who、what、where、when、why、how（包含 how much、how many），以獲得大意，而文章主旨常是測驗題目的第一題。接下來，建議先略讀所有的測驗問題，除了考主旨的題目外，其他問題通常為特定性題目，不外乎是要測驗文中的細節，要回答這些題目，並不需細讀全文，只要掌握測驗題目中的關鍵字：who、what、where、when、why、how（包含 how much、how many），即可就特定搜尋目標快速掃讀全文，獲得答案。

有時候這些特定性題目還包括單字字義和推論性問題，通常只要掃讀到文中這個資訊出現的地方，然後在上下文中稍加推論即可得到答案。

☆※ 小叮嚀：因為這個英文測驗答錯不倒扣分數，所以若不知正確答案，也應隨意選個答案，不要不答。

例：

Scotland Yard first began to use dogs for police work in 1946. At that time, they used only four dogs. Today, more than 300 police dogs are working in London. When a young dog is three months old, it goes to the home of a policeman. This person will be the dog's "handler." The dog stays at its handler's home, lives with his family, and plays with the children. A handler must really know his dog.

1. How old is a dog when it goes to its handler's home?
A. Three months old.
B. Six months old.
C. Nine months old.
D. One year old.　（正確答案：A）

解析：

這一題的題目問的是 "how old"，快速瀏覽選項，即可得知是在問 "how many months old"，以此資訊掃描全文，馬上可以得到答案。

2. What is the article mainly about?

A. Policemen.

B. Police dogs.

C. Handlers.

D. Scotland Yard.　（正確答案：B）

解析：

　　這是在測驗全文的大意，而本文的第一句即是主題句，由此即可得到全文主旨，若是不放心的話，可以再快速瀏覽一下內文來確定答案。

☆結論：

　　希望本書的讀者能夠靈活運用以上的技巧，這樣不但可以大幅提高全民英檢這個項目中的分數，也可以在實際生活中看到自己英語閱讀能力的進步，而英語閱讀理解力進步對於英語寫作有非常直接的幫助。

中級 Reading & Writing

NEW

新制全民英檢

GEPT

The General English Proficiency Test [Intermediate]

閱讀&寫作 模擬試題+解答

CHAPTER 3

寫作講座

中級 Reading & Writing

NEW

新制全民英檢

GEPT

The General English Proficiency Test [Intermediate]

閱讀&寫作 模擬試題 +解答

1. 平日培養英語寫作能力的方法

　　以下是一些值得推薦的準備方法：

　　☆多閱讀，尤其是優良的英文讀物或教材，熟悉實用的單字、片語，甚至句子出現的上下文，靈活運用於自己的寫作中。

　　☆先從養成寫作習慣開始，把握練習英文寫作的機會，例如用英文來寫臉書、電子郵件、日記等等，遇到不確定如何表達時，勤查字典或請教高手以學習正確用法。

　　☆練習用英文寫整段的文章，掌握英文寫作要領，先寫主旨句再發展要點或列舉例證。

　　☆由段落發展至整篇的文章，勤加練習組織段落成為一篇完整的文章架構，若是論說文，通常是先點出主題，之後舉例或以要點說明，最後總結論；若是敘述文，則通常是按照發生時間順序來發展文章，經常用所得到的教訓和結論收尾。

2. 如何針對全民英檢中級寫作作準備

本測驗共有兩部分。第一部份為中譯英,第二部份為英文作文。測驗時間為 40 分鐘。題目及說明皆印在試卷上,答案請寫在寫作能力測驗答案紙上。各部份採整體式評分 (0~5 級分),再轉換成百分制。評分重點包括內容、組織、文法結構、用字遣詞、標點符號、大小寫等。

中級 Reading & Writing

NEW

新制全民英檢

GEPT

The General English Proficiency Test | Intermediate |

閱讀&寫作 模擬試題 +解答

第一部分：中譯英 (40%)

請將下列的一段中文翻譯成通順、達意且前後連貫的英文。

☆準備方法：

中譯英這個部分不會很難，準備要訣是平時就要多儲備實用的單字和片語，多練習翻譯，例如英文課本或英文學習雜誌上的翻譯練習，還有平時查字典時看到的常用例句，都是隨手可得的練習材料。除此之外，平時多要求自己在腦中練習用英語來表達，甚至養成不時練習從中文翻譯成英文的習慣，都會對中譯英這個部分助益良多。

第二部分：英文作文 (60%)

請依下面所提供的文字提示寫一篇英文作文，長度約 120 字（8 至 12 個句子）。作文可以是一個完整的段落，也可以分段。

☆準備方法：

英文作文這個項目的要訣很簡單，首先要記住一點：不需要用到非常艱深的字彙，尤其在不確定用法和正確拼字的情況下，寧可用有把握的表達方式。除此之外，還要控制好時間，讓寫出來的短文不但結構完整而且邏輯清楚。平時多閱讀全民英檢優良作文範例和評論，經常規定自己在時間限制下練習寫作文，並且請老師或高手批改和評分，長久下來，在考場下筆時就會有如神助。

➡寫作能力測驗分數說明

中級 Reading & Writing
NEW
新制全民英檢
GEPT
The General English Proficiency Test [Intermediate]
閱讀&寫作 模擬試題 +解答

第一部分：中譯英 (40%)

級分	分數	説明
5	40	內容能充分表達題意，文段 (text) 結構及連貫性甚佳。用字遣詞、文法、拼字、標點及大小寫幾乎無誤。
4	32	內容適切表達題意，句子結構及連貫性大致良好。用字遣詞、文法、拼字、標點及大小寫偶有錯誤，但不妨礙題意之表達。
3	24	內容未能完全表達題意，句子結構鬆散，連貫性不足。用字遣詞及文法有誤，但不妨礙題意之表達，且拼字、標點及大小寫也有錯誤。
2	16	僅能局部表達原文題意，句子結構不良、有誤，且大多難以理解並缺乏連貫性。字彙有限，文法、拼字、標點及大小寫有許多錯誤。
1	8	內容無法表達題意，語句沒有結構概念及連貫性，無法理解。字彙極有限，文法、拼字、標點及大小寫之錯誤多且嚴重。
0	0	未答 / 等同未答。

寫作講座

第二部分：英文作文 (60%)

級分	分數	說明
5	40	內容適切表達題目要求，組織甚佳，靈活運用字彙及句型，句型有變化，文法、拼字或標點符號無重大錯誤。
4	32	內容符合題目要求，組織大致良好，正確運用字彙及句型，文法、拼字或標點符號鮮有重大錯誤。
3	24	內容大致符合題目要求，但未完全達意，組織尚可，能夠運用的字彙有限，文法、拼字、標點符號有誤。
2	16	內容未能符合題目要求，大多難以理解，組織不良，能夠運用的字彙有限，文法、拼字、標點符號有許多錯誤。
1	8	內容未能符合題目要求，完全無法理解，沒有組織，能夠運用的 字彙有限，文法、拼字、標點符號有過多錯誤。
0	0	未答 / 等同未答。

☆計分說明：

「全民英檢」寫作能力測驗採人工閱卷，每位考生的作答均由二位評分人員分別經初、複審程序評定級分，所評之級分經平均後，再轉換為百分制報分。

中級 Reading & Writing
新制全民英檢
GEPT
The General English Proficiency Test | Intermediate |
NEW

閱讀&寫作 模擬試題+解答

☆分數計算公式如下：

【(第一部分第一位評分人員評定之級分＋第一部分第二位評分人員評定之級分)÷2 ×20分 ×40%】＋【(第二部分第一位評分人員評定之級分＋第二部分第二位評分人員評定之級分)÷2 ×20分 ×60%】

假設某考生兩部分得分為：第一部分中譯英一位人員評為4級分、一位評分人員評為5級分，第二部分英文作文一位評分人員評分為4級分、一位人員評分為4級分，經平均後轉換為百分制為84分(【(4級分＋5級分)÷2 ×20分 ×40%】＋【(4級分＋4級分)÷2 ×20分 ×60%】＝36分＋48分＝84分)。

CHAPTER

4

閱讀模擬試題

※ 本章共包含三回閱讀模擬試題

中級 Reading & Writing

新制全民英檢

GEPT

The General English Proficiency Test | Intermediate |

NEW

閱讀&寫作 模擬試題 +解答

第一回閱讀模擬試題

英語能力分級檢定測驗中級

閱讀能力測驗

　　本測驗分三部份，全為四選一之選擇題，每部份各 15 題，共 45 題。本測驗總分 100 分，平均每題 2.2 分，作答時間 45 分鐘。

第一部分：詞彙和結構

　　本部份共 15 題，每題有一個空格。請就試題冊上提供的 A、B、C、D 四個選項中選出最適合題意的字或詞，標示在答案紙上。

例：

After the police arrive, they will begin to interview the people who _____ in the jewelry store at the time of the robbery.

A. have been

B. will be

C. were

D. are

正確答案為 C，請在答案紙上塗黑作答。

1. Those who _____ the test do not have to do this homework.
   A. is passing
   B. passed
   C. to pass
   D. passing

2. That new teacher really knows how to _____ students, so all students like him.

中級 Reading & Writing
新制全民英檢
NEW
GEPT
The General English Proficiency Test | Intermediate |
閱讀&寫作 模擬試題 +解答

A. make friends with

B. look down upon

C. think about

D. get away with

3. This new medicine _____ saved his life.

   A. openly

   B. lively

   C. tightly

   D. miraculously

4. My younger brother _____ English in order to have more time to study history and geography.

   A. looked up

   B. held up

   C. gave up

   D. took care

5. Up till now, I _____ any European country.

   A. have never been to

   B. had been to

   C. will go to

   D. was going

6. We _____ go on a cycling tour during summer vacation when I
was small.
   A. often
   B. used to
   C. are used to
   D. were

7. You should schedule your activities _____ your time.
   A. according to
   B. due to
   C. as a result of
   D. thanks to

8. Make sure that all the books you borrowed _____ to the library
by the end of this semester.
   A. returned
   B. has returned
   C. are returned
   D. return

9. All students _____ to visit the Science Museum during this
coming winter vacation.
   A. expecting
   B. who expect

中級 Reading & Writing

新制全民英檢

GEPT

The General English Proficiency Test [Intermediate]

閱讀&寫作 模擬試題 +解答

NEW

C. to expect

D. are expected

10. He _____ finished this project on time if he had not taken a
Christmas break.

A. should

B. would have

C. will have

D. shall have

11. _____ children grow up, they tend to want more personal space
than before.

A. For

B. As

C. To

D. There

12. All of the refreshments have been _____ by the volunteers for
this activity.

A. taken care of

B. watched out for

C. checked into

D. looked into

13. Currently, many exhibitions of Buddhist Art _____ in the
galleries in Taiwan.
   A. are held
   B. hold
   C. will hold
   D. holding

14. On Chinese New Year's Eve, all family members get _____ for a
reunion dinner.
   A. up
   B. away
   C. out
   D. together

15. Those _____ are ill know the importance of health.
   A. whose
   B. who
   C. whom
   D. when

第二部分：段落填空

　　本部份共 15 題，包括二至三個段落，每個段落各含 5 個空格。請就試題冊上提供的 A、B、C、D 四個選項中選出最適合題意的字或詞，標示在答案紙上。

　　例：

Susan had a terrible day today. First she (1) up by a strange phone call at four o'clock this morning. When she was about to (2) the receiver, the phone stopped ringing. Then, she got up late and (3) the company bus, so she was thirty minutes late for work, (4) made her boss very angry. What was (5) , when she got home this afternoon, she couldn't open the door because she had left her keys at her office.

1. A. woke

　 B. was woken

　 C. wakes

　 D. is awake

　 (正確答案：B)

2. A. pick up

　 B. pick

　 C. pick at

D. pick on

（正確答案：A）

3. A. dropped

   B. lost

   C. missed

   D. left

   （正確答案：C）

4. A. that

   B. this

   C. what

   D. which

   （正確答案：D）

5. A. harder

   B. worse

   C. later

   D. angrier

   （正確答案：B）

Questions 16-20

How to be a good host depends a lot on the guests. Some guests expect the hosts to (16) them up at the airport and accompany them during the whole tours; others prefer to travel by themselves. To some guests, accomodation provided by the hosts would be appreciated, while quite a few guests would (17) stay in a hotel. It is important to ask politely what your guests want to do in the first place and schedule the travel plans accordingly. (18) speaking, young backpackers tend to travel without much planning, and they do not like to be expected to (19) in social gatherings during their stay beforehand. With Smart Phones and other electronic gadgets, young travelers become more (20) than ever in their travels.

16. A. take
    B. grow
    C. get
    D. pick

17. A. like
    B. rather

C. dislike

D. choose

18. A. Generously

    B. Generally

    C. Personally

    D. Wonderfully

19. A. put off

    B. apply for

    C. take up

    D. show up

20. A. mobile

    B. wealthy

    C. priceless

    D. important

Questions 21-25

Gift giving is often much more complicated than most people think. Sometimes, a good gift can improve friendship, while a bad gift shows the (21) of the gift-giver. Many people give vouchers as gifts when they have

中級 Reading & Writing
新制全民英檢
GEPT
The General English Proficiency Test [Intermediate]
NEW

閱讀&寫作 模擬試題 +解答

(22) gift ideas. Some people prefer to make the gifts (23) ,such as scarves and gloves, to show their warm thoughts. It is important to know your gift-receiver; (24) , you would not want to give sweets to a diabetic patient. Some people ask their friends in advance what they want to receive as gifts, but by (25) so, the surprise of gift-giving would be taken away.

21. A.picture
   B. affection
   C. carelessness
   D. greetings

22. A. run away from
   B. come down with
   C. get away with
   D. run out of

23. A. by themselves
   B. by oneself
   C. by the way
   D. by means of

24. A. to one's joy

B. to one's surprise

C. for example

D. as a result

25. A. making

B. wanting

C. letting

D. doing

第三部分：閱讀理解

本部份共 15 題，包括數段短文，每段短文後有 2~5 個相關問題，試題冊上均提供 A、B、C、D 四個選項，請由四個選項中選出最適合者，標示在答案紙上。

例：

Scotland Yard first began to use dogs for police work in 1946. At that time, they used only four dogs. Today, more than 300 police dogs are working in London. When a young dog is three months old, it goes to the home of a policeman. This person will be the dog's "handler." The dog stays at its handler's home, lives with his family, and plays with the children. A handler must really know his dog.

1. How old is a dog when it goes to its handler's home?

A. Three months old.

B. Six months old.

C. Nine months old.

D. One year old.

(正確答案：A)

2. What is the article mainly about?

A. Policemen.

B. Police dogs.

C. Handlers.

D. Scotland Yard.

(正確答案：B)

Questions 26-28

Track**02**

In recent years, traditional Chinese medicine has been popular and recognized internationally. Acupunture treatments and herbal medicine have helped many patients very much in relieving their pain. It is widely believed that Chinese medicine is very mild, compared to western pharmacy. Quite a few doctors trained in western medicine have started to study Chinese medicine. Sometimes they give prescription of herbs to their patients. One of the characteristics of Chinese medicine is that it is natural and can be taken as nutritious supplements. In fact, many soups we eat in winter contain medicinal ingredients. Nowadays it is not unusual for patients to take Chinese herbs along with western medicine at the same time if their doctors allow them to do so.

26. What is the general topic of this short article?

A. nutrition

B. health food

C. Chinese medicine

D. doctors and clinics

27. The word "relieving" is closest in meaning to

A. taking

B. easing

C. lighting

D. examining

28. What does the writer imply in this passage?

A. Western doctors do not recognize Chinese medicine at all.

B. Chinese medicine can work along with western medicine.

C. Patients are not willing to take Chinese medicine.

D. Western medicine is milder than herbal medicine.

Track**03**

Questions 29-31

Right now, smoking in restaurants and closed public areas is not

allowed in Taiwan. In most public places, such as train stations, the smoking ban sign can be seen almost everywhere. Many cafés and restaurants provide special areas for smokers, usually somewhere outdoors. In some public parks, special booths are set for smokers to smoke in. Some smokers feel they are discriminated against because they are separated from others. Not all places have special space for smokers to smoke in. Many health-conscious people will ask smokers to put out their cigarettes. Although most smokers can understand the purpose of smoking regulations is to promote health, most of them still prefer to smoke freely.

29. What is the main idea of this passage?

A. Smoking and writing.

B. Smoking among teenagers.

C. Smoking-related issues.

D. Smoking in schools.

30. According to the passage, how do some smokers feel about smoking regulations?

A. They feel happy about them.

B. They feel they are discriminated against.

C. They cannot understand the need of these regulations.

D. They decide to quit smoking because of these regulations.

31. What does "health-conscious" most likely mean here?

A. Working in hospitals.

B. Making smoking regulations.

C. Giving tickets for smoking.

D. Caring for health.

Track**04**

Questions 32-34

From: James Johnson

To: Da-de Lee

Subject: Thank you for hosting us in Taiwan

Date: Friday, January 3, 2014 10:04:31 a.m.

Dear Da-de,

During our 2-week stay in Taiwan in December last year, you and your baseball team members did a great job hosting us in Taiwan. All of our team members were very grateful for the effort you put in.

Because of you, we could focus on playing baseball and exchanging valuable experiences of the game. Besides, with your company we had a good time doing sightseeing in Taiwan.

We sincerely hope all of you can have the opportunity of visiting us

in the States so that we could host you in return. Thank you again for your help.

Best Regards,

_____

James Johnson

Baseball Team of Seattle High School

Email: jamesjohnsonyahoo.com

Website: http://www.baseballseattle.com/

32. What is the main purpose of this e-mail?

A. To apologize.

B. To express gratitude.

C. To update information.

D. To notify changes.

33. Beside the baseball game, what does the writer of this e-mail especially want to thank the receiver for?

A. For arranging meetings for them.

B. For driving them around.

C. For showing them around.

D. For cooking meals for them.

34. What does the the writer of this e-mail want to do for the receiver in return?

A. Hosting him in America.

B. Taking him to NBA games.

C. Treating him fantastic meals.

D. Introducing him to local teams.

Questions 35-37

Track**05**

Most students in Taiwan do not like to speak up in class because they are not used to speaking in public. In adult life, people cannot avoid doing public speaking completely; therefore, we should train ourselves to speak in public as often as we can. One of the common issues many inexperienced speakers have is the fear of making mistakes in front of others. To combat this fear, you can visilize giving a successful speech and repeat this image several times in the head. When the time of speaking comes, the brain will automatically recall the scene. In this way, it is much more likely to succeed as a great public speaker than before.

35. What is the main idea of this passage?

A. Public speaking is very hard to master.

B. Students do not have to speak up.

C. The key to speaking successfully in public.

D. Nobody can cure the fear of speaking in public.

36. According to this passage, what is the main problem of
    the beginners of public speaking?

A. They do not have much in common with the listeners.

B. They are afraid to make a fool of themselves in public.

C. They often make mistakes in their language.

D. They do not understand the need of their listeners.

37. What is recommended for the inexperienced public speakers to
    do in order to conquer their fear?

A. To memorize all the content of the speech.

B. To write down main points to remind themselves.

C. To listen to the advice of experienced speakers.

D. To picture themselves as successful speakers.

Track06

Questions 38-40

In order to achieve success, it is very important to set goals. This is true not only in studies but also in career. Some people prefer not to be bound by goals, and they often wander off with little success. With no special directions, they end up wasting much time and efforts. In contrast, those who concentrate on achieving their goals are more likely to succeed. Some people set unrealistic goals, such as learning to speak Japanese in three weeks. Not surprisingly, these people always become very disappointed with themselves in the end. To set reasonable goals, we should have a clear understanding of ourselves and the resources around us. When we focus on our goals with proper timetables, we will be delightfully surprised at our potential finally.

38. What is the main topic of this passage?

A. Different people have different goals.

B. Setting goals is very important for success.

C. Some people cannot set goals in learning.

D. People without goals are happy with themselves.

39. Which of the following is NOT one of the problems of those who do not set goals?

A. They waste time and efforts.

B. They are very flexible at work.

C. Their cannot focus on their work.

D. They cannot reach their goals.

40. According to this passage, what should we pay special attention to

 in setting our goals?

A. We should let people around us know our goals.

B. We should compare our goals with others.

C. We should not change our goals too often.

D. Our goals should be realistic and achievable.

GEPT 中級閱讀測驗
模擬試題第一回解答

1. B	11. B	21. C	31. D
2. A	12. A	22. D	32. B
3. D	13. A	23. A	33. C
4. C	14. D	24. C	34. A
5. A	15. B	25. D	35. C
6. B	16. D	26. C	36. B
7. A	17. B	27. B	37. D
8. C	18. B	28. B	38. B
9. D	19. D	29. C	39. B
10.B	20. A	30. B	40. D

第一回閱讀模擬試題解答與翻譯

1. Those who _____ the test do not have to do this homework.

A. is passing

B. passed

C. to pass

D. passing

那些 _____ 考試的人不用寫家庭作業。

A. pass 的現在進行式

B. pass 的過去式

C. pass 的動詞原形，也就是不定式

D. pass 的現在分詞

正確答案：B

☆解題關鍵

在這裡要測驗的是動詞的正確時態，根據句意，應該是指通過考試的人，所以選項 B：passed（pass 的過去式）是唯一的正確選項。

2. That new teacher really knows how to _____ students, so all students like him.

A. make friends with

B. look down upon

C. think about

D. get away with

那位新老師很懂得和學生 _____，所以所有的學生都喜歡他。

A. 做朋友

B. 瞧不起

C. 思考

D. 逃過

正確答案：A

☆解題關鍵

這一題要測驗的是片語的用法，根據句意，只有選項 A：make friends with（做朋友）符合整句話的意思。

3. This new medicine _____ saved his life.

A. openly

B. lively

C. tightly

D. miraculously

這個新藥 ＿＿＿＿＿ 救了他一命。

A. 公開地

B. 活潑地

C. 緊密地

D. 奇蹟似地

正確答案：D

☆解題關鍵

在這裡需要選一個最合適的副詞，而四個選項皆為副詞，比較字義後，只有選項 D：miraculously（奇蹟似地）符合句意。

4. My younger brother ＿＿＿＿＿ English in order to have more time to study history and geography.

A. looked up

B. held up

C. gave up

D. took care

我弟弟為了有更多的時間來讀歷史和地理，＿＿＿＿＿ 了英文。

A. 查詢

B. 支撐

C. 放棄

D. 照顧

正確答案：C

☆解題關鍵

這裡要選擇一個適合的片語，四個選項皆為片語，而且皆為常見的片語，但是只有選項 C：gave up（give up 的過去式），放棄，符合句意。

5. Up till now, I _____ any European country.

A. have never been to

B. had been to

C. will go to

D. was going

到目前為止，我 _____ 到過任何歐洲國家。

A. 從未去過

B. 從前去過

C. 將會去

D. 過去正要去

正確答案：A

☆解題關鍵

此處要測驗的是時態的正確用法，因為句中出現 "up till now"，表示至今的經驗，所以要使用現在完成式，選項 A：have never been to。其中 "never" 和 "any" 經常同時出現。

6. We _____ go on a cycling tour during summer vacation
   when I was small.
   A. often
   B. used to
   C. are used to
   D. were

小時候我們 _____ 暑假騎單車去旅行。
A. 經常
B. 過去經常
C. 現在習慣
D. are 的過去式

中級 Reading & Writing
新制全民英檢
GEPT
The General English Proficiency Test [Intermediate]
閱讀&寫作 模擬試題 +解答
NEW

正確答案：B

☆解題關鍵

因為句中有 "when I was small"，所以只有表示過去動作的用法才符合句意，分析所有選項，選項 A 與 C 皆會使前半句變為現在式，所以不正確，而選項 D 雖為過去式，但放在句中，不合正確動詞用法，所以不選。正確答案為選項 B：used to（過去經常；曾經）附帶一提的是，選項 C：are used to：現在習慣，用法為 are used to V-ing，例如：He is used to getting up early.（他習慣早起。）

7. You should schedule your activities _____ your time.
A. according to
B. due to
C. as a result of
D. thanks to

你應該 _____ 你的時間來安排活動。
A. 依據
B. 因為
C. 歸因於
D. 因為

正確答案：A

☆解題關鍵

這裡要測驗的是片語用法，而所有選項皆為介系詞片語，因此必須由後面所接的名詞（your time）來判斷前面應該要用的正確片語。分析所有選項，只有選項 A 符合句意，為正確答案。而選項 B 和選項 D 皆表示「因為」的意思，在一個題目中不可能有兩個同義選項是正確答案。

8. Make sure that all the books you borrowed _____ to the library by the end of this semester.

A. returned

B. has returned

C. are returned

D. return

學期結束前一定要將所有你借的書 _____ 給圖書館。

A. return 的過去式（歸還了）

B. return 的第三人稱現在完成式（已歸還了）

C. return 的被動式（被歸還）

D. return 的動詞原形（歸還）

Reading & Writing

NEW

中級
新制全民英檢
GEPT
The General English Proficiency Test [Intermediate]

閱讀&寫作 模擬試題
+解答

正確答案：C

☆解題關鍵
　　時態的問題在這部分很常見，只要有清楚觀念即可正確作答，因為題目中明顯告知在 **"Make sure"** 之後是由 **"that"** 引導的子句，所以只有選項 C：are returned（被歸還）才能使整個句子完整。

　　9. All students _____ to visit the Science Museum during this coming winter vacation.

A. expecting

B. who expect

C. to expect

D. are expected

　　所有的學生在即將到來的這個寒假中都 _____ 參觀科學博物館。

A. 期待中

B. 期待的

C. 期待

D. 必須

正確答案：D

☆解題關鍵

雖然四個選項皆含 expect，但是只有選項 D 合乎句意和文法，因為 "are expected to" 字面上的意思是「被期待要做某件事」，也就是「必須」的意思。而其他選項皆不能構成完整句子，因為不合文法。

10. He _____ finished this project on time if he had not

taken a Christmas break.

A. should

B. would have

C. will have

D. shall have

要是他聖誕節那時沒有休假的話，他 _____ 及時完成這個案子了。

A. 應該

B. 應該就能夠

C. 將會

D. 將會

正確答案：B

☆解題關鍵

　　假設語氣的用法經常出現於各類英語考試中，因為這是基本而常用的句型。由句子的後半部可以判斷出，這是與過去事實相反的假設用法，而答案只有一個可能，就是選項 B：would have，表示「那時候應該就能夠」。

11. _____ children grow up, they tend to want more personal space than before.

A. For

B. As

C. To

D. There

_____ 小孩長大，他們傾向於想要更多的私人空間。

A. 為了

B. 隨著

C. 給予

D. 那邊

正確答案：B

☆解題關鍵
這裡是測驗 ”as” 作為連接詞的用法，意思是「隨著」。

12. All of the refreshments have been _____ by the volunteers for this activity.

A. taken care of

B. watched out for

C. checked into

D. looked into

這個活動的志工 _____ 所有的點心。

A. 負責

B. 留心

C. 調查

D. 研究

正確答案：A

☆解題關鍵

　　這幾個選項的片語當中，只有選項 A："taken care of"：負責，合乎句意，"take care of" 除了「負責」外，還有「照顧」的意思，例如：Take care of these children.（好好照顧這些小孩。）其他片語也很常見，不妨一起背下來：watch out for：留心；check into：調查；look into：調查，研究。

13. Currently, many exhibitions of Buddhist Art _____ in the galleries in Taiwan.
A. are held
B. hold
C. will hold
D. holding

目前有許多佛教藝術文物在台灣的美術館展出。
A. hold 的現在被動式
B. hold 的動詞原形
C. hold 的未來式
D. hold 的現在分詞

正確答案：A

☆解題關鍵

因為有 "currently"（目前），表示要用現在式，而且主詞為物品，要用被動式，所以正確的時態應該是現在被動式，答案為選項 A：are held：被舉辦。

14. On Chinese New Year's Eve, all family members get _____ for a reunion dinner.

A. up

B. away

C. out

D. together

在農曆除夕夜，所有家庭成員都 _____ 吃團圓飯。

A. 起床

B. 走開

C. 外出

D. 聚集

正確答案：D

☆解題關鍵

動詞後面加上不同的副詞，意思也就經常完全不同，這裡只有選項 D：get together（聚在一起）適合句中情境。

15. Those _____ are ill know the importance of health.

A. whose

B. who

C. whom

D. when

那些生病的人知道健康的重要性。

A. 他們的

B. ... 的人

C. who 的受詞

D. 當

正確答案：B

☆解題關鍵

"who" 作為關係代名詞時，緊接在表示人的名詞（此處，"those" 等於 "those people"：「那些人」）之後，表示「... 的人」，所以選項為 B。

第二部分：段落填空

本部份共 15 題，包括二至三個段落，每個段落各含 5 個空格。請就試題冊上提供的 A、B、C、D 四個選項中選出最適合題意的字或詞，標示在答案紙上。

例：

Susan had a terrible day today. First she (1) up by a strange phone call at four o'clock this morning. When she was about to (2) the receiver, the phone stopped ringing. Then, she got up late and (3) the company bus, so she was thirty minutes late for work, (4) made her boss very angry. What was (5) , when she got home this afternoon, she couldn't open the door because she had left her keys at her office.

1. A. woke
   B. was woken
   C. wakes
   D. is awake
   (正確答案：B)

2. A. pick up
   B. pick
   C. pick at

中級 Reading & Writing

新制全民英檢

GEPT

NEW

閱讀&寫作 模擬試題 +解答

The General English Proficiency Test | Intermediate |

D. pick on

（正確答案：A)

3. A. dropped

   B. lost

   C. missed

   D. left

（正確答案：C)

4. A. that

   B. this

   C. what

   D. which

（正確答案：D)

5. A.harder

   B. worse

   C. later

   D. angrier

（正確答案：B)

Questions 16-20

How to be a good host depends a lot on the guests. Some guests expect the hosts to (16) them up at the airport and accompany them during the whole tours; others prefer to travel by themselves. To some guests, accomodation provided by the hosts would be appreciated, while quite a few guests would (17) stay in a hotel. It is important to ask politely what your guests want to do in the first place and schedule the travel plans accordingly. (18)speaking, young backpackers tend to travel without much planning, and they do not like to be expected to (19)in social gatherings during their stay beforehand. With Smart Phones and other electronic gadgets, young travelers become more (20) than ever in their travels.

中譯

　　如何才能當個好主人，主要看客人而定。有的客人期待主人到機場接機，並且全程陪他們同遊；而有的客人則比較喜歡自由行。有的客人喜歡主人提供住宿，而不少客人則比較喜歡待在旅館。很重要的是，先有禮地問客人，他們想要做的事物，然後依此來安排旅遊計劃。通常來説，年輕的背包客旅行時傾向於不做太多計劃，而且不喜歡事先被要求於停留期間出席社交場合。有了智慧型手機和其他電子用品，年輕的遊客旅行時變得比從前更加機動了。

16. A. take　拿

中級 Reading & Writing
新制全民英檢
GEPT
The General English Proficiency Test [Intermediate]

NEW

閱讀&寫作 模擬試題 +解答

B. grow　生長

C. get　取得

D. pick　接

17. A. like　喜歡

　　B. rather　較

　　C. dislike　不喜歡

　　D. choose　選擇

18. A. Generously　慷慨地

　　B. Generally　通常地

　　C. Personally　私人地

　　D. Wonderfully　美好地

19. A. put off　延期

　　B. apply for　申請

　　C. take up　接下

　　D. show up　出現

20. A. mobile　機動的

　　B. wealthy　富有的

　　C. priceless　無價的

　　D. important　重要的

正確答案：16.(D) 17.(B) 18.(B) 19.(D) 20.(A)

➥重要字彙和片語

☆ pick somebody up = pick up somebody 接
例：His mother always picks him up at 5 o'clock.
他的母親總是在五點來接他。

☆ would rather 寧願
用法：
would rather + 原形動詞
例：I would rather stay home and watch TV.
我寧願在家看電視。

☆ prefer to 更喜歡
用法如下：
prefer to + 原形動詞 + rather than + 原形動詞
或
prefer to + 原形動詞 + instead of + 動名詞
例：I prefer to work rather than do nothing.

= I prefer to work instead of doing nothing.

比起什麼都不做，我寧願工作。

另一用法：

prefer + 名詞／動名詞 + to + 名詞／動名詞

例：

I prefer juice to tea.

我喜歡果汁勝於茶。

I prefer singing to dancing.

和跳舞比起來，我比較喜歡唱歌。

☆ generally speaking 通常來說

副詞加上 speaking，便成了常見的副詞片語，例如：frankly speaking, honestly speaking 皆是「坦白地說」的意思。

Questions 21-25

Gift giving is often much more complicated than most people think. Sometimes, a good gift can improve friendship, while a bad gift shows the (21) of the gift-giver. Many people give vouchers as gifts when they have (22) gift ideas. Some people prefer to make the gifts (23) ,such as scarves and gloves, to show their warm thoughts. It is important to know your gift-receiver; (24) , you would not want to give sweets to a diabetic patient. Some people ask their friends in advance what they want to receive as gifts, but by (25) so, the surprise of gift-giving would be taken away.

中譯

送禮物常常比大多數人想的還要複雜。一個好的禮物有時候可以增進友誼,而一個不好的禮物則顯示出了送禮者的粗心。很多人想不出來要送什麼的時候,就送禮卷。有的人比較喜歡自己做禮物來表現他們的溫情,像是圍巾和手套。重要的是要了解收你禮物的人;例如,你不會想要送糖尿病患者甜點。有的人會事先問他們的朋友想要什麼當禮物,但是這樣做也就沒有送禮的驚喜了。

21. A.picture　身影

　　B.affection　喜愛

　　C.carelessness　疏忽

　　D.greetings　祝福

22. A.run away from　逃跑

　　B.come down with　生病

　　C.get away with　避開

　　D.run out of　用完

23. A.by themselves　靠自己（複數）

B.by oneself　獨自（單數）

C.by the way　順便

D.by means of　藉著

24. A.to one's joy　令某人歡喜

B.to one's surprise　令某人驚喜

C.for example　例如

D.as a result　結果

25. A.making　製作

B.wanting　想要

C.letting　讓

D.doing　做

正確答案：21.(C)　22.(D)　23.(A)　24.(C)　25.(D)

➥重要字彙和片語

☆ run out of 用完，耗盡

例：We have run out of time. Let's call it a day.

我們已經沒有時間了。今天就到此為止。

☆ in advance 預先

例：He booked a room in the hotel in advance.

他先訂好了飯店的一個房間。

第三部分：閱讀理解

　　本部份共 15 題，包括數段短文，每段短文後有 2~5 個相關問題，試題冊上均提供 A、B、C、D 四個選項，請由四個選項中選出最適合者，標示在答案紙上。

　　例：

Scotland Yard first began to use dogs for police work in 1946. At that time, they used only four dogs. Today, more than 300 police dogs are working in London. When a young dog is three months old, it goes to the home of a policeman. This person will be the dog's "handler." The dog stays at its handler's home, lives with his family, and plays with the children. A handler must really know his dog.

1. How old is a dog when it goes to its handler's home?

A. Three months old.

B. Six months old.

C. Nine months old.

D. One year old.

(正確答案：A)

2. What is the article mainly about?

A. Policemen.

B. Police dogs.

C. Handlers.

D. Scotland Yard.

(正確答案：B)

Questions 26-28

In recent years, traditional Chinese medicine has been popular and recognized internationally. Acupunture treatments and herbal medicine have helped many patients very much in relieving their pain. It is widely believed that Chinese medicine is very mild, compared to western pharmacy. Quite a few doctors trained in western medicine have started to study Chinese medicine. Sometimes they give prescription of herbs to their patients. One of the characteristics of Chinese medicine is that it is natural and can be taken as nutritious supplements. In fact, many soups we eat in winter contain medicinal ingredients. Nowadays it is not unusual for patients to take Chinese herbs along with western medicine at the same time if their doctors allow them to do so.

最近幾年來，中藥越來越受歡迎，也越受到世界各國的承認。針灸和草藥醫學幫助了很多病患減輕疼痛。一般認為，相較於西醫，中醫非常溫和。不少學西醫的醫生已開始學習中醫，他們有時候開草藥處方給病人。中藥的特徵之一是成份天然，可以當作營養補品食用。事實上，很多我們冬天所喝的湯中含有藥材。現在病人服用草藥來搭配西藥已經不是罕見情形，前提是他們的醫生許可他們這麼做。

26. What is the general topic of this short article?

A. nutrition

B. health food

C. Chinese medicine

D. doctors and clinics

這篇短文的主旨為何？

A. 營養

B. 健康食品

C. 中醫

D. 醫生與病人

27. The word "relieving" is closest in meaning to

A. taking

B. easing

C. lighting

D. examining

"relieving" 這個字和下列哪個字義最相近？

A. 服用

B. 減輕

C. 照明

D. 檢查

28. What does the writer imply in this passage?

A. Western doctors do not recognize Chinese medicine at all.

B. Chinese medicine can work along with western medicine.

C. Patients are not willing to take Chinese medicine.

D. Western medicine is milder than herbal medicine.

作者在這篇文章暗示什麼？

A. 西方的醫生完全不承認中醫

B. 中醫可以和西醫相輔相成

C. 病人不願意服用中藥

D. 西藥比草藥還溫和

正確答案：26.(C) 27.(B) 28.(B)

Questions 29-31

Right now, smoking in restaurants and closed public areas is not allowed in Taiwan. In most public places, such as train stations, the smoking ban sign can be seen almost everywhere. Many cafés and restaurants provide special areas for smokers, usually somewhere outdoors. In some public parks, special booths are set for smokers to smoke in. Some smokers feel they are discriminated against because they are separated from others. Not all places have special space for smokers to smoke in. Many health-conscious people will ask smokers to put out of their cigarettes. Although most smokers can understand the purpose of smoking regulations is to promote health, most of them still prefer to smoke freely.

目前在台灣的餐廳和密閉公共區域，抽菸是不合法的。在大部分公眾場所，例如火車站，禁止吸菸的標誌幾乎到處可見。很多咖啡屋和餐廳提供特別區域給吸菸者，通常為戶外地區。某些公共公園設有給吸菸者在內抽菸的特別吸菸棚。有些吸菸者覺得他們受到了歧視，因為他們被迫和其他人隔離。並不是所有的地方都有給吸菸者抽菸的特別空間。很多注重健康的人會要求吸菸者將菸熄掉。雖然大部分的吸菸者可以明白吸菸法規的目的是為了提昇健康，大多數抽菸的人還是比較喜歡能自由自在吸菸。

29. What is the main idea of this passage?

A. Smoking and writing.

B. Smoking among teenagers.

C. Smoking-related issues.

D. Smoking in schools.

這篇文章的大意為何？

A. 吸菸與寫作

B. 青少年吸菸問題

C. 與吸菸相關的議題

D. 在校園內吸菸

30. According to the passage, how do some smokers feel about smoking regulations?

A. They feel happy about them.

B. They feel they are discriminated against.

C. They cannot understand the need of these regulations.

D. They decide to quit smoking because of these regulations.

中級 Reading & Writing

NEW

新制全民英檢

GEPT

The General English Proficiency Test [Intermediate]

閱讀&寫作 模擬試題 +解答

根據這篇文章，吸菸者覺得吸菸法規怎麼樣？

A. 他們感到很高興

B. 他們感到被歧視

C. 他們不能理解這些法規存在的必要性

D. 他們因為這些法規決定要戒菸

31. What does "health-conscious" most likely mean here?

A. Working in hospitals.

B. Making smoking regulations.

C. Giving tickets for smoking.

D. Caring for health.

「注重健康」在這裡最有可能是什麼意思？

A. 在醫院工作

B. 制定吸菸法規

C. 開抽菸罰單

D. 關心健康

正確答案：29.(C) 30.(B) 31.(D)

Questions 32-34

From: James Johnson

To: Da-de Lee

Subject: Thank you for hosting us in Taiwan

Date: Friday, January 3, 2014 10:04:31 a.m.

Dear Da-de,

During our 2-week stay in Taiwan in December last year, you and your baseball team members did a great job hosting us in Taiwan. All of our team members were very grateful for the effort you put into.

Because of you, we could focus on playing baseketball and exchanging valuable experiences of the game.Besides, with your company we had a good time doing sightseeing in Taiwan.

We sincerely hope all of you can have the opportunity of visiting us in the States so that we could host you in return. Thank you again for your help.

Best Regards,

————————————

James Johnson

Baseball Team of Seattle High School

Email: jamesjohnsonyahoo.com

Website: http://www.baseballseattle.com/

From: 詹姆斯 · 強森

To: 李達德

Subject: 謝謝在台灣的招待

Date:2014 年一月三日 星期五 10:04:31 a.m.

達德：

　　去年十二月我們待在台灣的兩個星期內，你和你們棒球隊隊員對我們招待非常周到。我們所有的隊員都非常感謝你們所投注的心力。

　　因為有你們，我們才能夠專心在球場上打棒球還有交流寶貴經驗。除此之外，有你們的陪伴，我們才能在台灣盡情觀光。

　　我們誠心希望你們能有機會來美國拜訪我們，好讓我們有機會回報你們的招待。再度謝謝你們的幫忙。

　　敬祝安康

　　――――――――

　　詹姆斯 · 強森

　　西雅圖高中棒球隊

　　Email: jamesjohnsonyahoo.com

　　Website: http://www.baseballseattle.com/

32. What is the main purpose of this e-mail?

A. To apologize.

B. To express gratitude.

C. To update information.

D. To notify changes.

這封電子郵件的主旨是什麼？

A. 道歉

B. 致謝

C. 更新資訊

D. 通知變更

33. Beside the baseball game, what does the writer of this -mail especially want to thank the receiver for?

A. For arranging meetings for them.

B. For driving them around.

C. For showing them around.

D. For cooking meals for them.

除了棒球賽外，寫這封電子郵件的人特別還要謝謝收信人什麼？

A. 替他們安排會議

B. 為他們開車

C. 帶他們到處參觀

D. 為他們煮飯

34. What does the the writer of this e-mail want to do for

the receiver in return?

A. Hosting him in America.

B. Taking him to NBA games.

C. Treating him fantastic meals.

D. Introducing him to local teams.

寫這封電子郵件的人想要怎麼樣回報收信人？

A. 在美國招待他

B. 帶他去看 NBA 球賽

C. 請他吃美食

D. 介紹他到當地球隊

正確答案：32.(B) 33.(C) 34.(A)

Questions 35-37

Most students in Taiwan do not like to speak up in class because they are not used to speaking in public. In adult life, people cannot avoid doing public speaking completely; therefore, we should train ourselves to speak in public as often as we can. One of the common issues many inexpereiced speakers have is the fear of making mistakes in front of others. To combat this fear, you can visilize giving a successful speech and repeat this image several times in the head. When the time of speaking comes, the brain will automatically recall the scene. In this way, it is much more likely to succeed as a great public speaker than before.

大部分的台灣學生不喜歡在課堂上發表意見，因為他們不習慣在公開場合說話。人長大後很難完全避開公眾演講，因此，我們應該盡可能練習公眾演說。很多缺乏經驗的演說者會有的問題是，害怕在別人面前犯錯。要克服這種恐懼，你可想像自己正在發表一場成功的演講，然後在腦中多次重覆這個景象。當演講的時機到時，頭腦就會自動叫出這個場景。這樣一來，成為成功公眾演說家的可能性就比從前高得多了。

35. What is the main idea of this passage?

A. Public speaking is very hard to master.

B. Students do not have to speak up.

C. The key to speaking successfully in public.

中級 Reading & Writing
NEW
新制全民英檢
GEPT
The General English Proficiency Test [Intermediate]
閱讀&寫作 模擬試題 +解答

D. Nobody can cure the fear of speaking in public.

這段文章的主旨是什麼？
A. 公眾演説很難掌握
B. 學生不必發表意見
C. 在公開場合成功演説的要訣
D. 沒有人能治癒公眾演説的恐懼

36. According to this passage, what is the main problem of the beginners of public speaking?

A. They do not have much in common with the listeners.

B. They are afraid to make a fool of themselves in public.

C. They often make mistakes in their language.

D. They do not understand the need of their listeners.

根據這篇文章，剛開始公眾演説的人的主要問題為何？
A. 他們和聽眾沒有太多交集
B. 他們害怕在眾人前出醜
C. 他們經常犯語言錯誤
D. 他們不明白聽眾的需求

37. What is recommended for the inexperienced public speakers to do in order to conquer their fear?

A. To memorize all the content of the speech.

B. To write down main points to remind themselves.

C. To listen to the advice of experienced speakers.

D. To picture themselves as successful speakers.

這裡建議缺乏經驗的演說者如何擊退恐懼？

A. 背下全部演講內容

B. 寫下重點來提醒自己

C. 聽有經驗的演說家的建議

D. 想像自己是成功的公眾演說家

正確答案：35.(C) 36.(B) 37.(D)

Questions 38-40

In order to achieve success, it is very important to set goals. This is true not only in studies but also in career. Some people prefer not to be bound by goals, and they often wander off with little success. With

no special directions, they end up wasting much time and efforts. In contrast, those who concentrate on achieving their goals are more likely to succeed. Some people set unrealistic goals, such as learning to speak Japanese in three weeks. Not surprisingly, these people always become very disappointed with themselves in the end. To set reasonable goals, we should have a clear understanding of ourselves and the resources around us. When we focus on our goals with proper timetables, we will be delightfully surprised at our potential finally.

　　為了成功，設定目標非常重要，這一點在學業上和在職場上都是如此。有些人比較不喜歡被目標綁住，這些人通常到處晃散，達不到什麼成果。沒有特別的目標，這些人最後浪費了很多時間和心力。相反的，那些專注於達成目標的人較容易成功。有些人設定的目標不切實際，像是三個星期學會說日語。難怪這些人最後總是對自己很灰心。為了要設定合理的目標，我們要清楚了解我們自己和周圍的資源。如果我們專心朝向附有合理時間表的目標前進，最後我們會對自己的潛能感到驚喜。

38. What is the main topic of this passage?

A. Different people have different goals.

B. Setting goals is very important for success.

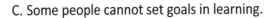

C. Some people cannot set goals in learning.

D. People without goals are happy with themselves.

這篇文章的主題為何？

A. 不同人有不同的目標

B. 設定目標對成功很重要

C. 有些人在學習時沒有辦法設定目標

D. 沒有目標的人對自己滿意

39. Which of the following is NOT one of the problems of those who do not set goals?

A. They waste time and efforts.

B. They are very flexible at work.

C. Their cannot focus on their work.

D. They cannot reach their goals.

下列哪一項不是沒有設定目標的人的問題？

A. 他們浪費時間和心力

B. 他們在職場很有彈性

C. 他們無法專心做他們的工作

D. 他們無法達成他們的目標

40. According to this passage, what should we pay special attention to in setting our goals?

A. We should let people around us know our goals.

B. We should compare our goals with others.

C. We should not change our goals too often.

D. Our goals should be realistic and achievable.

根據這篇文章，我們設定目標的時候應該特別注意什麼？

A. 我們應該讓周圍的人知道我們的目標

B. 我們應該和別人比較我們的目標

C. 我們不該太常改變我們的目標

D. 我們的目標應該實際且可達成

正確答案：38.(B) 39.(B) 40.(D)

第二回閱讀模擬試題

英語能力分級檢定測驗中級

閱讀能力測驗

　　本測驗分三部份，全為四選一之選擇題，每部份各 15 題，共 45 題。本測驗總分 100 分，平均每題 2.2 分，作答時間 45 分鐘。

第一部分：詞彙和結構

本部份共15題，每題有一個空格。請就試題冊上提供的A、B、C、D四個選項中選出最適合題意的字或詞，標示在答案紙上。

例：

After the police arrive, they will begin to interview the people who
_____ in the jewelry store at the time of the robbery.

A. have been

B. will be

C. were

D. are

正確答案為 C，請在答案紙上塗黑作答。

1. _____ wants to go to the concert, please sign up in the official
   website.
   A. Whatever
   B. Whoever
   C. Wherever
   D. However

2. Where _____ all these years?

    A. are you

    B. were you

    C. have you been

    D. will you be

3. Do you know _____ to do if somebody next to you has an accident?

    A. when

    B. where

    C. what

    D. who

4. Ms. Chen is _____ the media department in this company.

    A. in place of

    B. in the name of

    C. in the front of

    D. in charge of

5. When some people are under tremendous _____ , they sometimes break down.

    A. stress

    B. protection

    C. defense

    D. admiration

6. Do you usually _____ goals for English learning?

    A. take care

    B. rule out

    C. make sure

    D. set up

7. I saw him _____ with an English native speaker when I entered the room.

    A. talking

    B. was talking

    C. talked

    D. is talking

8. So far, I have never _____ my Englsh homework late.

    A. handed down

    B. handed over

    C. handed out

    D. handed in

9. _____ is the best attitude to communicate with people because everyone likes a nice and honest person.

    A. Success

    B. Sincerity

C. Intelligence

D. Diligence

10. You have to be _____ when you deal with money.

A. stressful

B. interesting

C. careful

D. forgiving

11. Brothers and sisters should _____ each other, and the whole family will be united.

A. be free of

B. take care of

C. look down upon

D. be reminded of

12. What _____ to the drawing you did last week? You're supposed to hand it in today.

A. will happen

B. happening

C. happen

D. happened

中級 Reading & Writing
新制全民英檢
GEPT
The General English Proficiency Test [Intermediate]
NEW
閱讀&寫作 模擬試題 +解答

13. People who are _____ appreciate what others have done for them.
    A. hard-working
    B. honest
    C. grateful
    D. careful

14. Technological _____, such as Smart Phone, have revolutionized our ways of living.
    A. inventions
    B. medication
    C. furniture
    D. spaceship

15. If I _____ one summer in the States last year, my English would have become fantastic.
    A. will spend
    B. spent
    C. had spent
    D. spend

第二部分：段落填空

本部份共 15 題，包括二至三個段落，每個段落各含 5 個空格。請就試題冊上提供的 A、B、C、D 四個選項中選出最適合題意的字或詞，標示在答案紙上。

例：

Susan had a terrible day today. First she (1) up by a strange phone call at four o'clock this morning. When she was about to (2) the receiver, the phone stopped ringing. Then, she got up late and (3) the company bus, so she was thirty minutes late for work, (4) made her boss very angry. What was (5) , when she got home this afternoon, she couldn't open the door because she had left her keys at her office.

1. A. woke
   B. was woken
   C. wakes
   D. is awake
   (正確答案：B)

2. A. pick up
   B. pick
   C. pick at

中級 Reading & Writing
新制全民英檢
GEPT
The General English Proficiency Test | Intermediate |
NEW
閱讀&寫作 模擬試題 +解答

D. pick on

（ 正確答案：A)

3. A. dropped

B. lost

C. missed

D. left

（ 正確答案：C)

4. A. that

B. this

C. what

D. which

（ 正確答案：D)

5. A. harder

B. worse

C. later

D. angrier

（ 正確答案：B)

Questions 16-20

Many parents want their children to take (16) in many extracurricular activities, such as dancing, learning a music instrument and so on. These courses not only take up much time (17) cost a lot of money. No all children are that (18) in what their parents want them to learn. For example, many people took piano lessons when they were very small, but only very few of them continued to play the piano when they grew up. Nowadays parents pay much more (19) to their children's interests then before. More and more kids are (20) to develop their hobbies and talents.

16. A. time
    B. part
    C. role
    D. effort

17. A. as well
    B.but also
    C.too
    D.rather

18. A. surprised
    B. disencouraged

C. interested

D. asked

19. A. attention

   B. time

   C. money

   D. leisure

20. A. distracted

   B. disappointed

   C. considered

   D. encouraged

Questions 21-25

Religion is not taught in most schools, and most teachers usually do not talk about their own religions in class, either. While young people are (21) to choose their own religions, most students simply (22) their parents' footsteps in their spiritual lives. In fact, most people do not have sufficient knowledge of religions. Because of frequent church activities, Christianity is (23) spread. Recently, Buddhists are also quite active in promoting their religious (24) . Almost all religions teach people to help each (25) , and promote harmony in the whole society.

21. A. interested
    B. supposed
    C. focused
    D. disappointed

22. A. run
    B. get
    C. take
    D. follow

23. A. widely
    B. openly
    C. commonly
    D. symbolically

24. A. fables
    B. beliefs
    C. questions
    D. justice

25. A. the other
    B. another
    C. one
    D. other

第三部分：閱讀理解

　　本部份共 15 題，包括數段短文，每段短文後有 2~5 個相關問題，試題冊上均提供A、B、C、D 四個選項，請由四個選項中選出最適合者，標示在答案紙上。

例：

Scotland Yard first began to use dogs for police work in 1946. At that time, they used only four dogs. Today, more than 300 police dogs are working in London. When a young dog is three months old, it goes to the home of a policeman. This person will be the dog's "handler." The dog stays at its handler's home, lives with his family, and plays with the children. A handler must really know his dog.

1. How old is a dog when it goes to its handler's home?

A. Three months old.

B. Six months old.

C. Nine months old.

D. One year old.

(正確答案：A)

2. What is the article mainly about?

A. Policemen.

B. Police dogs.

C. Handlers.

D. Scotland Yard.

(正確答案：B)

Questions 26-28

Jan 8, 2014

Volunteers Needed

   We are now seeking volunteers who are willing to help the elderly in the Sunshine Nursing Home during this coming winter vacation. There will be lunches and dinners provided for the volunteers, and the general duties are not heavy:

   Talking with the elderly

   Doing gentle excercises with the elderly

   Calling the nurses if necessary

   Writing reports by the end of the shift

The applicants do not have to be any special majors, but they should be patient, caring and sociable. If you're interested, please contact Ms. Lin (lilylin@hotmail.com) as soon as possible. The elderly there need your help urgently. Thank you very much.

26. What is the purpose of this notice?

A. To seek attention

B. To seek the elderly

C. To seek volunteers

D. To seek employment

27. Which of the following is NOT included in the general duties?

A. Writing reports about the elderly

B. Writing letters for the elderly

C. Chatting with the elderly

D. Working out with the elderly

28. What is required for the applicants?

A. Students of Nursing Department.

B. Music and language thrapists.

C. Experienced certified nurses.

D. Kind and sociable people.

Questions 29-31

In recent years, overwrieght children have become an obvious problem in Taiwan. Many parents blame the American fast food chain stores for this, but they themelves have seldom taught their children how to keep a balanced diet. As a result, many school kids with obesity have to go to expensive weight losing programs. It is indeed a complete change of lifestyle to go on a diet. Not all people can manage to achieve their goals of weight loss. Thus it's important to set feasible goals in order to keep motivated during the whole process. Whatever parents decide to do to help their overweight children, they should take them to see a doctor first.

Track**08**

29. What is the main topic of this passage?

A. What students have for lunch.

B. How to help obese children.

C. What to buy to prepare meals.

D. What to order in a fast food store.

中級 Reading & Writing
新制全民英檢
GEPT
The General English Proficiency Test [Intermediate]

NEW

閱讀&寫作 模擬試題 +解答

30. The word **"feasible"** is closest in meaning to

A. doable

B. affordable

C. curable

D. treatable

31. According to this passage, who should parents take their overweight children to visit for advice to go on a diet?

A. Personal trainers

B. Gym managers

C. Medical doctors

D. School teachers

Questions 32-34

Track09

There are some golden rules to follow in preparing for an English test: First, find out what the test is made of, for example, listening comprehension and composition writing and so on. When you study for the test, do as many practice tests as possible to familiarize yourself with the test. Pay special attention to the mistakes you made before. Study good compositions in English textbooks. You can invite your friends to

form a small study group and quiz each other. What is also important is to schedule the time properly. Do not stay up late to study the night before the test, so that the next day you will have a clear mind to do your best in the English test.

32. What is the general topic of this passage?

A. How to speak English fluently.

B. How to prepare for an English test.

C. How to write a composition.

D. How to find an English study group.

33. What is recommended to do as a first step in preparing for an English test?

A. Find out what the test consists of.

B. Write many practice e-mails.

C. Work on listening comprehension.

D. Memorize good English compositions.

34. According to this passage, what should people NOT do before taking an English test?

A. Doing many practice tests.

中級 Reading & Writing

NEW

新制全民英檢

GEPT

The General English Proficiency Test [Intermediate]

閱讀&寫作 模擬試題 +解答

B. Finding out the test format.

C. Forming a study group.

D. Going to bed late to study.

Questions 35-37

Track **10**

Please join us to learn more about health issues! The health lecuture series will be provided every other two Saturdays from 3:00 to 5:00 in the afternoon in the conference room. Tickets are free but a reservation is necessary. We will invite doctors as well as medical researchers to give speeches on a wide range of health issues. Please check our Facebook page to find out about the coming talks. The next lecture will focus on the health care of the elderly. At the end of each talk, Q & A sessions will follow to let listeners have a discussion with speakers. If you have special topics you would like us to cover, please let us know.

35. What is the purpose of this notice?

A. To provide the care of the elderly.

B. To open a discussion in a conference.

C. To announce the news of health lectures.

D. To look into the mind of the medical staff.

36. How can people attend the health lectures?

A. People can attend the health lectures if they buy tickets.

B. People can attend the health lectures if they know the staff.

C. People can attend the health lectures if they are members of F acebook.

D. People can attend the health lectures if they book in advance.

37. What will be covered in the Q & A sessions?

A. Open dialogs and interaction.

B. Refreshments and drinks.

C. Special issues and next topics.

D. Medication and nutrition.

Questions 38-40

Nowadays Facebook seems to become a must among people of all generations. One major concern of those who do not want to use Facebook is the privacy issue. They are afraid of their private photos to be circulated and used for wrong purposes. Many people who used to criticize Facebook now become Facebook users. The reason behind it is quite simple: It's

Track **11**

中級 Reading & Writing
NEW
新制全民英檢
GEPT
The General English Proficiency Test [Intermediate]
閱讀&寫作 模擬試題 +解答

because most of their friends are Facebook users. In order to keep in touch with their friends at home and abroad, they have to catch up with this powerful social media. Just like almost everything else, Facebook can be used both in positive and in negative ways. One of the serious problems with Facebook is online bullying. Parents and teachers are especially cautious of the impacts Facebook has on their teenagers.

38. What is the main idea of this passage?

A. Facebook and its inventor.

B. Facebook and its impacts.

C. Facebook and marketing.

D. Facebook and other social media.

39. According to this passage, what is the major concern of people who do not use Facebook?

A. Interruption at work.

B. Friends' gossips

C. Unwanted advertisements.

D. The problems with privacy.

40. According to this passage, what is one of the serous problems among Facebook teenage users?

A. They might become addicted to the Internet.

B. They might be bullied by other Facebook users.

C. They might start a gossip about their teachers.

D. They might be cheated of their money by others.

中級 Reading & Writing
新制全民英檢
GEPT
The General English Proficiency Test [Intermediate]

NEW

閱讀&寫作 模擬試題 +解答

GEPT 中級閱讀測驗
模擬試題第二回解答

1. B	11. B	21. B	31. C
2. C	12. D	22. D	32. B
3. C	13. C	23. A	33. A
4. D	14. A	24. B	34. D
5. A	15. C	25. D	35. C
6. D	16. B	26. C	36. D
7. A	17. B	27. B	37. A
8. D	18. C	28. D	38. B
9. B	19. A	29. B	39. D
10C	20. D	30. A	40. B

第二回閱讀模擬試題解答與翻譯

本測驗分三部份，全為四選一之選擇題，每部份各 15 題，共 45 題。本測驗總分 100 分，平均每題 2.2 分，作答時間 45 分鐘。

第一部分：詞彙和結構

本部份共 15 題，每題有一個空格。請就試題冊上提供的 A、B、C、D 四個選項中選出最適合題意的字或詞，標示在答案紙上。

例：

After the police arrive, they will begin to interview the people who
_____ in the jewelry store at the time of the robbery.

A. have been

B. will be

C. were

D. are

正確答案為 C，請在答案紙上塗黑作答。

1. _____ wants to go to the concert, please sign up in
   the official website.
A. Whatever
B. Whoever
C. Wherever
D. However

_____ 想要去聽音樂會的人，請到官網上登記。
A. 任何什麼
B. 任何…的人
C. 任何…的地方
D. 無論如何

正確答案：B

☆解題關鍵

在 what、who、where、how 後面加上 "ever"，成了 "whatever、

whoever、wherever、however"，就是原義加上了「任何」的意思，成了「任何什麼」、「任何…的人」、「任何…的地方」、「無論如何」的意思。在這裡要表達的是「任何想要去聽音樂會的人」，所以答案為選項 B。

2. Where _____ all these years?
A. are you
B. were you
C. have you been
D. will you be

這些年來你都在哪裡？
A.are you 的動詞原形
B.are you 的過去式
C.are you 的現在完成式
D.are you 的未來式

正確答案：C

☆解題關鍵

因為句中有 **"all these years"**，因此時態要使用現在完成式：**"have you been"**，表示從過去到現在之意。

3. Do you know _____ to do if somebody next to you has an accident?

A. when

B. where

C. what

D. who

如果你周圍的人發生意外了，你知道要 _____ 嗎？

A. 什麼時候

B. 什麼地方

C. 什麼

D. 誰

正確答案：C

☆解題關鍵

按照句意，「如果你周圍的人發生意外了」，後面應該要加「你知道要『做什麼』嗎？」，所以答案為選項 C：”what” to do。

4. Ms. Chen is _____ the media department in this company.

A. in place of

B. in the name of

C. in the front of

D. in charge of

陳先生 _____ 這家公司的媒體部門。

A. 取代

B. 以…為名

C. 在…之前

D. 負責

正確答案：D

☆解題關鍵

此處測驗片語用法，可由選項 D 中的 ”charge”：「責任；任務」，推測出 ”in charge of” 為「負責」之意。

中級 Reading & Writing
新制全民英檢
NEW
GEPT
The General English Proficiency Test [Intermediate]
閱讀&寫作 模擬試題 +解答

5. When some people are under tremendous _____ , they sometimes break down.

A. stress

B. protection

C. defense

D. admiration

有些人在巨大的 _____ 下有時會崩潰。

A. 壓力

B. 保護

C. 防禦

D. 仰慕

正確答案：A

☆解題關鍵

根據句意，此處符合的答案只有選項 A：stress，壓力。"under stress" 為一個常見片語，意思為「處在壓力下」。

6. Do you usually _____ goals for English learning?

A. take care

B. rule out

C. make sure

D. set up

你通常會 _____ 學英文的目標嗎？

A. 照料

B. 排除

C. 確定

D. 設定

正確答案：D

☆解題關鍵

根據句意，此處符合的答案是選項 D：set up：設定。而選項 A 的片語正確用法為 "take care of"：照料；選項 D 的片語正確用法為 "make sure of"：確定。

7. I saw him _____ with an English native speaker when I entered

中級 Reading & Writing
新制全民英檢
GEPT
The General English Proficiency Test [Intermediate]
NEW
閱讀&寫作 模擬試題 +解答

the room.

A. talking

B. was talking

C. talked

D. is talking

我進門的時候看見他在和一位英語母語者 _____。

A. talk 的現在分詞

B. talk 的過去進行式

C. talk 的過去式

D. talk 的現在進行式

正確答案：A

☆解題關鍵

看見某人正在做什麼事情，要用現在分詞表達某人正在進行的動作，而 talk 的現在分詞是 talking。

8. So far, I have never _____ my Englsh homework late.

A. handed down

B. handed over

C. handed out

D. handed in

至今我從來沒有遲 _____ 過我的英文作業。

A. 發下

B. 轉交

C. 分發

D. 繳交

正確答案：D

☆解題關鍵

　　以 "hand" 為首的片語很多，所以在學習的時候就要將加上不同介系詞的 "hand" 片語與其正確用法一起學好。正確答案為選項 D：hand in：繳交，通常都是用在地位較低者繳交東西給地位較高者的情形，例如此處為學生交作業給老師。

9. _____ is the best attitude to communicate with people because everyone likes a nice and honest person.

A. Success

B. Sincerity

C. Intelligence

D. Diligence

_____ 是和人溝通時最好的態度，因為每個人都喜歡親切又誠實的人。

A. 成功

B. 誠懇

C. 聰慧

D. 勤勉

正確答案：B

☆解題關鍵

這個句子的後半部分其實就是所缺單字的解釋，所以答案很清楚是選項 B：Sincerity：誠懇。

10. You have to be _____ when you deal with money.

A. stressful

B. interesting

C. careful

D. forgiving

你在處理金錢的時候要 _____ 。

A. 有壓力的

B. 有意思的

C. 謹慎的

D. 寬容的

正確答案：C

☆解題關鍵

在這個情形中，四個選項內，適用的形容詞只有選項 C：careful：小心謹慎。

11. Brothers and sisters should _____ each other, and the whole family will be united.

A. be free of

B. take care of

C. look down upon

D. be reminded of

兄弟姊妹應該要互相 _____ ，全家才能團結。

A. 無…的

B. 照顧

C. 輕視

D. 被提醒

正確答案：B

☆解題關鍵

這個句子前後有因果關係，為了要達到全家團結的結果，那麼兄弟姊妹應該要互相照顧。在四個選項中，答案只能是選項 B：take care of：照顧。

12. What _____ to the drawing you did last week? You're supposed to hand it in today.

A. will happen

B. happening

C. happen

D. happened

你上星期畫的素描 _____ 怎麼了？本來今天你得要交上來的。

A. happen 的未來式

B. happening 的現在分詞

C. happen 的動詞原形

D. happened 的過去式

正確答案：D

☆解題關鍵

　　這一類時態的問題，只要細讀到時間副詞，例如此處的 ”last week”，即可判斷出應該是要用過去式，再加上後面的句子提供的資訊，答案就很明白了。

13. People who are _____ appreciate what others have done for them.

A. hard-working

B. honest

中級 Reading & Writing
新制全民英檢
GEPT
The General English Proficiency Test [Intermediate]
NEW
閱讀&寫作 模擬試題 +解答

C. grateful

D. careful

_____ 的人感激別人為他們所做的事情。

A. 工作勤勞的

B. 誠實的

C. 感恩的

D. 細心的

正確答案：C

☆解題關鍵

這個句子的後半部 "appreciate what others have done for them."，也就是在解釋前面的答案 "grateful"： 感恩的。

14. Technological _____, such as Smart Phone, have revolutionized our ways of living.

A. inventions

B. medication

C. furniture

D. spaceship

科技 _____，例如智慧型手機，完全改變了我們的生活方式。
A. 發明物
B. 醫藥
C. 傢俱
D. 太空梭

正確答案：A

☆解題關鍵

空格後所舉的例子：智慧型手機，點出了正確答案的範疇。

15. If I _____ one summer in the States last year, my English would have become fantastic.
A. will spend
B. spent
C. had spent
D. spend

如果我去年在美國 _____ 一個夏天，我的英語那時就會變得好極了。

A. spend 的未來式

B. spend 的過去式

C. spend 的過去完成式

D. spend 的動詞原形

正確答案：C

☆解題關鍵

此處要測驗的是假設語氣的用法，因為是與過去事實相反，所以正確答案為選項 C：had spent。整句話的意思是，如果我去年在美國待上一個夏天，我的英語那時就會變得好極了。

第二部分：段落填空

本部份共 15 題，包括二至三個段落，每個段落各含 5 個空格。請就試題冊上提供的 A、B、C、D 四個選項中選出最適合題意的字或詞，標示在答案紙上。

例：

Susan had a terrible day today. First she (1) up by a strange phone call at four o'clock this morning. When she was about to (2) the receiver, the phone stopped ringing. Then, she got up late and (3) the company bus, so she was thirty minutes late for work, (4) made her boss very angry. What was (5) , when she got home this afternoon, she couldn't open the door because she had left her keys at her office.

1. A. woke

   B. was woken

   C. wakes

   D. is awake

   (正確答案：B)

2. A. pick up

   B. pick

   C. pick at

D. pick on

(正確答案：A)

3. A. dropped

B. lost

C. missed

D. left

(正確答案：C)

4. A. that

B. this

C. what

D. which

(正確答案：D)

5. A. harder

B. worse

C. later

D. angrier

(正確答案：B)

Questions 16-20

Many parents want their children to take (16) in many extracurricular activities, such as dancing, learning a music instrument and so on. These courses not only take up much time (17) cost a lot of money. No all children are that (18) in what their parents want them to learn. For example, many people took piano lessons when they were very small, but only very few of them continued to play the piano when they grew up. Nowadays parents pay much more (19) to their children's interests then before. More and more kids are (20) to develop their hobbies and talents.

中譯

很多家長要他們的孩子參加很多的課外活動，像是舞蹈、學樂器等等。這些課程不但很花時間，花費也很高。並非所有的小孩都對他們父母要他們學的東西那麼有興趣。舉例來說，很多人在小時候上過鋼琴課，但是只有極少數人長大後繼續彈鋼琴。現在的家長對他們孩子的興趣較從前更加注意。越來越多的小孩的興趣和天份受到鼓勵而得以發展。

NEW

中級 Reading & Writing

新制全民英檢

GEPT

The General English Proficiency Test [Intermediate]

閱讀&寫作 模擬試題 +解答

16. A. time　時間

　　B. part　部分

　　C. role　角色

　　D. effort　努力

17. A. as well　也

　　B. but also　也

　　C. too　也

　　D. rather　而是

18. A. surprised　驚訝的

　　B. disencouraged　氣餒的

　　C. interested　有興趣的

　　D. asked　要求的

19. A. attention　注意力

　　B. time　時間

　　C. money　金錢

　　D. leisure　閒暇

20. A. distracted　分心的

　　B. disappointed　失望的

　　C. considered　視為…的

D. encouraged　被鼓勵的

正確答案：16.(B) 17.(B) 18.(C) 19.(A) 20.(D)

➥ 重要字彙和片語

☆ take part in 參加

例：Nowadays boys can take part in cooking lessons, too.

現在男孩子也可以參加烹飪課。

☆ not only A but also B 不但 A，而且 B〔also 可以省略〕

（A 與 B 必須是對等的）

等同於有 as well 或 too 的句子

例：He speaks not only English but also Chinese.

他不但會說英語，也會說國語。

=He speaks English and Chinese as well.

=He speaks English as well as Chinese.

=He speaks English and Chinese, too.

Questions 21-25

Religion is not taught in most schools, and most teachers usually do not talk about their own religions in class, either. While young people are (21) to choose their own religions, most students simply (22) their parents' footsteps in their spiritual lives. In fact, most people do not have sufficient knowledge of religions. Because of frequent church activities, Christianity is (23) spread. Recently, Buddhists are also quite active in promoting their religious (24) . Almost all religions teach people to help each (25) and promote harmony in the whole society.

中譯

學校裡不教宗教,大部分老師通常也不在課堂上談論他們的宗教。照道理講,年輕人應該可以選擇自己的宗教,但是大部分學生在信仰上追隨父母的腳步。事實上,大多數人沒有足夠的宗教知識。因為教會活動很頻繁,基督教散布地很廣。最近佛教也在傳教方面很活躍。幾乎所有的宗教都教人要互相幫助並且提昇社會整體的和諧。

21. A. interested　有興趣的
　　B. supposed　應該的
　　C. focused　專注的
　　D. disappointed　失望的

22. A. run　跑
　　B. get　得到
　　C. take　取得
　　D. follow　追隨

23. A. widely　散布地
　　B. openly　公開地
　　C. commonly　平常地
　　D. symbolically　象徵地

24. A. fables　寓言
　　B. beliefs　信仰
　　C. questions　問題
　　D. justice　公正

25. A. the other　另一個人
　　B. another　其他的人
　　C. one　一個

D. other　其他

正確答案：21.(B)　22.(D)　23.(A)　24.(B)　25.(D)

➥重要字彙和片語

☆ be supposed to 應該

例：He is supposed to arrive at ten o'clock.

照道理講，他應該十點到達。

☆ because of 因為

用法：

後面要加名詞或動名詞，而 because 後面要加子句

例：Because of a car accident, he could not make it yesterday.

因為車禍，他昨天不能來。

=Because he had a car accident, he could not make it yesterday.

第三部分：閱讀理解

　　本部份共 15 題，包括數段短文，每段短文後有 2~5 個相關問題，試題冊上均提供 A、B、C、D 四個選項，請由四個選項中選出最適合者，標示在答案紙上。

　　例：

Scotland Yard first began to use dogs for police work in 1946. At that time, they used only four dogs. Today, more than 300 police dogs are working in London. When a young dog is three months old, it goes to the home of a policeman. This person will be the dog's "handler." The dog stays at its handler's home, lives with his family, and plays with the children. A handler must really know his dog.

1. How old is a dog when it goes to its handler's home?

A. Three months old.

B. Six months old.

C. Nine months old.

D. One year old.

（正確答案：A）

2. What is the article mainly about?

145

A. Policemen.

B. Police dogs.

C. Handlers.

D. Scotland Yard.

（正確答案：B)

Questions 26-28

Jan 8, 2014

Volunteers Needed

We are now seeking volunteers who are willing to help the elderly in the Sunshine Nursing Home during this coming winter vacation. There will be lunches and dinners provided for the volunteers, and the general duties are not heavy:

Talking with the elderly

Doing gentle excercise with the elderly

Calling the nurses if necessary

Writing reports by the end of the shift

The applicants do not have to be any special majors, but they should be patient, caring and sociable. If you're interested, please contact Ms. Lin (lilylinhotmail.com) as soon as possible. The elderly there need your help urgently. Thank you very much.

2014 年 1 月 8 日

徵求志工

我們正在尋找在這個即將到來的寒假中，願意來陽光銀髮族養護中心幫忙的志工。我們會提供午餐和晚餐給志工，而工作內容並不煩重：

— 與長者聊天
— 與長者做輕鬆的運動
— 需要時呼叫護士
— 在輪班工作時間結束前寫報告

申請者不需要有什麼特別的主修，但是必須有耐心，關心別人，有社交能力。如果您有興趣的話，請儘早聯絡林小姐 (lilylinhotmail.com)。這些長者急需您的幫助。非常感謝您。

26. What is the purpose of this notice?

A. To seek attention

B. To seek the elderly

C. To seek volunteers

D. To seek employment

這告示的目的是什麼？

A. 尋找注意力

B. 尋找長者

C. 尋找志工

D. 尋找工作機會

27. Which of the following is NOT included in the general duties?

A. Writing reports about the elderly

B. Writing letters for the elderly

C. Chatting with the elderly

D. Working out with the elderly

下列何者不包括在工作項目內？

A. 寫關於長者的報告

B. 為長者寫信

C. 與長者聊天

D. 與長者運動

28. What is required for the applicants?

A. Students of Nursing Department.

B. Music and language therapists.

C. Experienced certified nurses.

D. Kind and sociable people.

應徵者需要具備什麼條件？

A. 護理系的學生

B. 音樂和語言治療師

C. 有經驗的合格護士

D. 仁慈且有社交能力的人

正確答案：26.(C) 27.(B) 28.(D)

中級 Reading & Writing
新制全民英檢
GEPT
The General English Proficiency Test [Intermediate]
閱讀&寫作 模擬試題 +解答
NEW

Questions 29-31

In recent years, overwieght among children have become an obvious problem in Taiwan. Many parents blame the American fast food chain stores for this, but they themelves have seldom taught their children how to keep a balanced diet. As a result, many school kids with obesity have to go to expensive weight losing programs. It is indeed a complete change of lifestyle to go on a diet. Not all people can manage to achieve their goals of weight loss. Thus it's important to set feasible goals in order to keep motivated during the whole process. Whatever parents decide to do to help their overweight children, they should take them to see a doctor first.

最近幾年來，兒童過度肥胖在台灣已成為明顯問題。很多家長怪罪於美國速食連鎖店，但是他們自己本身很少教他們的小孩如何均衡飲食，結果很多肥胖的學齡兒童得要去上昂貴的減重課程。節食真的是生活方式的完全改變。並非所有人都能夠達到他們的減重目標。因此，為了要在整個過程中都保持鬥志，很重要的是，要設定可達成的目標。無論家長決定要如何幫助他們過重的孩子，都應該要先帶他們去看醫生。

29. What is the main topic of this passage?

A. What students have for lunch.

B. How to help obese children.

C. What to buy to prepare meals.

D. What to order in a fast food store.

這篇文章的主題是什麼？

A. 學生午餐吃些什麼

B. 如何幫助肥胖兒童

C. 該買些什麼來準備餐點

D. 在速食店該點什麼

30. The word "feasible" is closest in meaning to

A. doable

B. affordable

C. curable

D. treatable

"feasible" 這個字和哪個字的字義最相近？

A. 可行的

B. 負擔得起的

中級 Reading & Writing
新制全民英檢
GEPT
The General English Proficiency Test [Intermediate]
NEW
閱讀&寫作 模擬試題 +解答

C. 可治癒的

D. 可治療的

31. According to this passage, who should parents take their overweight children to visit for advice to go on a diet?

A. Personal trainers

B. Gym managers

C. Medical doctors

D. School teachers

根據這篇文章，家長要他們的過重孩子節食，應該要諮詢誰？

A. 私人教練

B. 健身中心經理

C. 醫生

D. 學校老師

正確答案：29.(B) 30.(A) 31.(C)

Questions 32-34

There are some golden rules to follow in preparing for an English test: First, find out what the test is made of, for example, listening comprehension and composition writing and so on. When you study for the test, do as many practice tests as possible to familiarize yourself with the test. Pay special attention to the mistakes you made before.Study good compositions in English textbooks. You can invite your friends to form a small study group and quiz each other. What is also important is to schedule the time properly. Do not stay up late to study the night before the test, so that the next day you will have a clear mind to do your best in the English test.

準備英文考試有些基本準則：首先，要了解考試的內容，例如：聽力測驗和作文等等。在做準備時，儘量多做模擬試題來熟悉考題。特別注意你從前犯過的錯誤，研讀英文課本裡的佳作文章。你可以邀請你的朋友和你一起組成學習小團體，彼此互相測驗。還有一點很重要，那就是要妥善安排時間。不要在考前一晚熬夜，這樣第二天你才能頭腦清楚地在英文考試中有最佳表現。

32. What is the general topic of this passage?

A. How to speak English fluently.

B. How to prepare for an English test.

C. How to write a composition.

D. How to find an English study group.

這篇文章的主題是什麼？

A. 如何將英語說得流利

B. 如何準備英文考試

C. 如何寫作文

D. 如何找英語學習團體

33. What is recommended to do as a first step in preparing for an English test?

A. Find out what the test consists of.

B. Write many practice e-mails.

C. Work on listening comprehension.

D. Memorize good English compositions.

這裡推薦準備英語考試的第一步為何？

A. 明白考試內容為何

B. 練習寫很多電子郵件

C. 加強聽力訓練

D. 熟背英文佳作文章

34. According to this passage, what should people NOT do before taking an English test?

A. Doing many practice tests.

B. Finding out the test format.

C. Forming a study group.

D. Going to bed late to study.

根據這篇文章，什麼是英文考試前不該做的？

A. 做很多模擬試題

B. 了解考題型式

C. 組成學習團體

D. 考前一晚熬夜

正確答案：32.(B) 33.(A) 34.(D)

Questions 35-37

Please join us to learn more about health issues! The health lecuture series will be provided every other two Saturdays from 3:00 to 5:00 in the afternoon in the conference room. Tickets are free but reservation is necessary. We will invite doctors as well as medical researchers to give speeches on a wide range of health issues. Please check our Facebook to find out the coming talks. Next lecture will focus on the health care of the elderly. At the end of each talk, Q & A sessions will follow to let listeners have a discussion with speakers. If you have special topics you would like us to cover, please let us know.

請和我們一起來多了解健康相關議題！這個健康講座系列每兩個星期六舉行一次，時間是下午三點到五點，地點在會議室。不需門票，但是必須預約。我們會邀請醫生以及醫學研究專家就各種主題的健康議題發表演講。請到我們臉書上查詢接下來的演講內容。下次的演講主要探討的是長者看顧議題。在每個演講結束後，會提供問答時間，來讓聽眾和演講者討論。如果你有特別想要我們討論的主題，請讓我們知道。

35. What is the purpose of this notice?

A. To provide the care of the elderly.

B. To open a discussion in a conference.

C. To announce the news of health lectures.

D. To look into the mind of the medical staff.

這告示的目的是什麼？

A. 提供長者的看護

B. 展開一場會議的討論

C. 宣布健康講座的消息

D. 探討醫療人員的心理

36. How can people attend the health lectures?

A. People can attend the health lectures if they buy tickets.

B. People can attend the health lectures if they know the staff.

C. People can attend the health lectures if they are members of Facebook.

D. People can attend the health lectures if they book in advance.

要如何才能參加健康講座？

A. 買票的人可以參加健康講座

中級 Reading & Writing
新制全民英檢
GEPT
The General English Proficiency Test [Intermediate]
NEW
閱讀&寫作 模擬試題 +解答

B. 認識工作人員的人可以參加健康講座

C. 臉書的成員可以參加健康講座

D. 提前預約的人可以參加健康講座

37. What will be covered in the Q & A sessions?

A. Open dialogs and interaction.

B. Refreshments and drinks.

C. Special issues and next topics.

D. Medication and nutrition.

問答時間中會包含什麼？

A. 公開對話和互動

B. 點心和飲料

C. 特別議題和下次主題

D. 醫療和營養

正確答案：35.(C) 36.(D) 37.(A)

Questions 38-40

Nowadays Facebook seems to become a must among people of all generations. One major concern of those who do not want to use Facebook is the privacy issue. They are afraid of their private photos to be circulated and used for wrong purposes. Many people who used to criticize Facebook now become Facebook users. The reason behind it is quite simple: It's because most of their friends are Facebook users. In order to keep in touch with their friends at home and abroad, they have to catch up with this powerful social media. Just like almost everything else, Facebook can be used both in positive and in negative ways. One of the serious problems with Facebook is online bullying. Parents and teachers are especially cautious of the impacts Facebook on their teenagers.

現在臉書似乎已成為各世代人的必備品。那些不使用臉書的人的主要考量是隱私權問題。他們擔心他們的私人照片會流傳開來而被不當使用。很多從前批評臉書的人現在卻變成臉書的使用者。背後的原因非常簡單：因為他們大部分的朋友使用臉書。為了要和他們國內外的朋友聯絡，他們必須要跟上潮流，使用這個有力的社群媒體。就像所有其他事物一樣，臉書有正面也有負面的用途。臉書的嚴重問題之一是網路霸凌。家長和老師對於臉書對青少年的影響特別謹慎小心。

中級 Reading & Writing
新制全民英檢
GEPT
The General English Proficiency Test [Intermediate]
NEW
閱讀&寫作 模擬試題 +解答

38. What is the main idea of this passage?

A. Facebook and its inventor.

B. Facebook and its impacts.

C. Facebook and marketing.

D. Facebook and other social media.

這篇文章的主旨為何？

A. 臉書與其發明者

B. 臉書與其影響

C. 臉書與行銷

D. 臉書與其他社群媒體

39. According to this passage, what is the major concern of people who do not use Facebook?

A. Interruption at work.

B. Friends' gossips

C. Unwanted advertisements.

D. The problems with privacy.

根據這篇文章，不使用臉書的人的主要考量是？

A. 工作受干擾

B. 朋友的八卦

C. 不想要的廣告

D. 隱私權問題

40. According to this passage, what is one of the serous problems

among Facebook teenage users?

A. They might become addicted to the Internet.

B. They might be bullied by other Facebook users.

C. They might start a gossip about their teachers.

D. They might be cheated of their money by others.

根據本篇文章，臉書的青少年使用者的嚴重問題之一是？

A. 他們可能會沉迷上網

B. 他們可能會被其他臉書使用者霸凌

C. 他們可能開始説他們老師的八卦

D. 他們可能會被其他人騙錢

正確答案：38.(B) 39.(D) 40.(B)

第三回閱讀模擬試題

英語能力分級檢定測驗中級

閱讀能力測驗

　　本測驗分三部份，全為四選一之選擇題，每部份各 15 題，共 45 題。本測驗總分 100 分，平均每題 2.2 分，作答時間 45 分鐘。

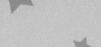
第一部分：詞彙和結構

本部份共 15 題，每題有一個空格。請就試題冊上提供的 A、B、C、D 四個選項中選出最適合題意的字或詞，標示在答案紙上。

例：

After the police arrive, they will begin to interview the people who _____ in the jewelry store at the time of the robbery.

A. have been

B. will be

C. were

D. are

正確答案為 C，請在答案紙上塗黑作答。

1. _____ did you celebrate your last birthday?

A. Who

B. What

C. How

D. Which

2. Mathmatics _____ his best subject in junior high school.

A. were

B. was

C. used to

D. are

3. We all _____ mistakes in our lives, but the important thing is not to repeat the same mistakes.

A. do

B. done

C. make

D. take

4. This is the place _____ I first met Ms. Lin seven years ago.

A. when

B. where

C. which

D. whose

5. The appointment was _____ because of her illness, and she hasn't felt better since then.

A. put away

B. put down

C. put out

D. put off

6. Do you usually buy your lunch or cook the meal _____?

A. by your mother

B. by yourself

C. by day

D. by you

7. Like most friends of mine, I _____ Chinese dishes to western food.

A. prefer

B. enjoy

C. cook

D. prepare

8. _____ do you think of the English final exam? Do you think it is too easy?

A. Which

B. When

C. What

D. Where

9. _____ is the best policy. I think we should tell the truth.

A. Success

中級 Reading & Writing

新制全民英檢

GEPT

The General English Proficiency Test [Intermediate]

NEW

閱讀&寫作 模擬試題 +解答

B. Happiness

C. Honesty

D. Diligence

10. Yesterday I caught a serious cold, but now I already feel much

_____.

A. caring

B. better

C. generous

D. moved

11. He is _____ of the teacher's eye, but many fellow students do
not like him.

A. apple

B. cake

C. sugar

D. sweets

12. He didn't sleep well last night, and _____, he failed the English
test this morning.

A. in agreement with

B. as a result

C. according to

D. as far as

13. Yesterday I had _____ much homework to do that I couldn't work out in the gym.

A. as

B. so

C. yet

D. more

14. Most young people like to study in a coeducational high school, _____ I prefer not.

A. when

B. so

C. but

D. what

15. No matter _____ you say, she will not forgive you.

A. when

B. what

C. whatever

D. whenever

第二部分：段落填空

本部份共 15 題，包括二至三個段落，每個段落各含 5 個空格。請就試題冊上提供的 A、B、C、D 四個選項中選出最適合題意的字或詞，標示在答案紙上。

例：

Susan had a terrible day today. First she (1) up by a strange phone call at four o'clock this morning. When she was about to (2) the receiver, the phone stopped ringing. Then, she got up late and (3) the company bus, so she was thirty minutes late for work, (4) made her boss very angry. What was (5) , when she got home this afternoon, she couldn't open the door because she had left her keys at her office.

1. A. woke

   B. was woken

   C. wakes

   D. is awake

   (正確答案：B)

2. A. pick up

   B. pick

   C. pick at

D. pick on

(正確答案：A)

3. A. dropped

B. lost

C. missed

D. left

(正確答案：C)

4. A. that

B. this

C. what

D. which

(正確答案：D)

5. A. harder

B. worse

C. later

D. angrier

(正確答案：B)

Questions 16-20

To most students in Taiwan, listening comprehension is the most difficult part of English tests. In fact, they can take (16) of media, such as radio broadcasting, TV news report and Internet resources, etc. In addition, they can listen to radio English learning programs. If they make an (17) to listen to English about 30 minutes a day, they can see great improvement. Some students (18) to watch movies in English to train their listening. The speed of dialogs in most movies is so fast that viewers have to (19) on the subtitles. In (20) to learn English effectively, most teachers recommend to use suitable matetials designed especially for learners.

16. A. care
    B. advantage
    C. use
    D. time

17. A. news
    B. effort
    C. work
    D. talent

18. A. prefer

    B. rather

    C. intend

    D. interest

19. A. attend

    B. repeat

    C. make

    D. rely

20. A. goal

    B. order

    C. purpose

    D. achievement

Questions 21-25

The umployment rate in Taiwan has in recent years risen tremendously. As a result, many college graduates have to (21) up jobs which did not require a college degree in the past, such as factory workers, taxi drivers and so on. Some say it is a waste of educational resources;

中級 Reading & Writing
NEW
新制全民英檢
GEPT
The General English Proficiency Test [Intermediate]
閱讀&寫作 模擬試題 +解答

(22) think that at least these overqualified people are not out of work. People who are out of (23) tend to create many problems for the society, especially young people who enter the job market for the first time. During the time of unemployment, the unemployed are suggested to take new courses to learn new skills, like computer softwares, and keep in (24) with people in their trades. Quite often, the employers and colleagues in the past can introduce new jobs to the (25) .

21. A. train
    B. obtain
    C. take
    D. get

22. A. others
    B. other
    C. another
    D. those

23. A. home
    B. meaning
    C. assigment
    D. employment

24. A. contact

B. conclusion

C. view

D. control

25. A. supervisors

B. job-seekers

C. human resources

D. outsourcing

NEW

中級 Reading & Writing
新制全民英檢
GEPT
The General English Proficiency Test [Intermediate]

閱讀&寫作 模擬試題 +解答

第三部分：閱讀理解

本部份共 15 題，包括數段短文，每段短文後有 2~5 個相關問題，試題冊上均提供 A、B、C、D 四個選項，請由四個選項中選出最適合者，標示在答案紙上。

例：

Scotland Yard first began to use dogs for police work in 1946. At that time, they used only four dogs. Today, more than 300 police dogs are working in London. When a young dog is three months old, it goes to the home of a policeman. This person will be the dog's "handler." The dog stays at its handler's home, lives with his family, and plays with the children. A handler must really know his dog.

1. How old is a dog when it goes to its handler's home?

A. Three months old.

B. Six months old.

C. Nine months old.

D. One year old.

(正確答案：A)

2. What is the article mainly about?

A. Policemen.

B. Police dogs.

C. Handlers.

D. Scotland Yard.

(正確答案：B)

Questions 26-28

More and more parents are concerned about the negative influences of violent computer games on their children. Of all the noticeable bad impacts of computer games, aggression is most worrying to parents and educational experts. It is no secret that gun shooting computer games are especially popular among boys and male teenagers. Many male students would rather spend hours playing computer games than do any other things in their free time. An increasing number of male teenagers are so addicted to computer games that their daily lives are being interfered with. Some parents still allow them to play computer games simply because they do not know how to deal with their kids if the computer games are taken away from them.

26. What is the main idea of this passage?

A. Computer games and their designers.

B. Computer games and their negative influences.

C. Computer game industry and its future.

D. Computer games and the social media.

27. What negative impact of computer games on children is most obvious?

A. Positive thinking.

B. Aggressive behavior.

C. Improved social skills.

D. Outgoing personality.

28. Why do many parents still allow their children to play computer games?

A. Their children are the designers of the games.

B. Their children do not have other hobbies.

C. Their children show improvements in the games.

D. Their children are addicted to computer games.

Questions 29-31

Track**13**

   Among Taiwanese university students, male and female students are about equal in numbers and in acheivements. Once they enter the job market, males dominate the leadership in almost all companies. Although many female employees think it is due to the unfair system of promotion, most leading women at the top level think it is women who stop themselves from going ahead. It is not uncommon to see female employees decline the chance of promotion because of family reasons. Males on the other hand seldom do the same. It shows clearly that many female employees do not think it is possible to have work family balance if they take up higher positions. Many women in the managerial roles encourage young female employees to be brave and to succeed in both career and in family.

29. What is this passage mainly about?

A. Housework for men and women.

B. Women at the workplace.

C. Female staff in a university.

D. Female graduates in the job market.

30. According to this passage, what stops most women from advancing in their careers?

A. The pressure from the decision-makers.

B. The males do not want female supervisors.

C. They do not have the motivation to succeed.

D. The limits they set for themselves.

31. What do many leading women want young female employees to do?

A. To believe they can have work family balance.

B. To go back to business schools to get MBA degrees.

C. To get to know more business contacts.

D. To focus on work and career development.

Track**14**

Questions 32-34

Since the middle of last December, many customers have been complaining about not receiving any products after they remitted the money to an online company. Many customers had collected all the money

from their acquaintances in order to get special discounts. Now they lost not only their own money but also others'. The business owners have disappeared for the last couple of weeks, and until now there is no sign of them showing up. It is estimated that they had collected more than one million Taiwan Dollars, and many customers believe it is an intended fraud. Quite a few consumer protection groups ask the customers to pay special attention to online shopping because such frauds are often not covered in our current laws.

32. What is the topic of this report?

A. A case of privacy in the Internet.

B. A case of business fraud in the Internet.

C. A case of virtual dating in the Internet.

D. A case of tax fraud in the Internet.

33. What does "others'" after "but also" mean here?

A. Other people's products.

B. Other people's reputation.

C. Other people's money.

D. Other people's packages.

34. Why do consumer protection groups ask the customers to pay special attention to online shopping?

A. Because of the prices of online products.

B. Because of the gray zone in online shopping

C. Because of the convenience of shopping.

D. Because of the privacy of online shopping.

Track**15**

Questions 35-37

Fairness is what most students require of their teachers, but most teachers find it extremely hard to achieve. In fact, in the experiences of almost all teachers, absolute objectivity is nearly impossible. The interaction that teachers have with their students in class leaves them with particular impressions of the students. Although all teachers try their best to be objective, teachers might give points based on their previous opinions about the students. To solve this problem, more people might be included in grading entrance exams. Experts who haven't met the students are frequently invited to judge students' presentations. Quite often the names of students are covered in order to help teachers remain objective in grading the papers.

35. What is the main topic of this passage?

A. Fair trading does not exist at all.

B. Objective grading is very common.

C. Teachers are not likely to be totally fair.

D. Students interfere with teachers' privacy.

36. According to this passage, why is it not easy for teachers to be completely fair and objective?

A. Most teachers have their opinions about their students.

B. Teachers do not know their students at all.

C. Most students do not respect their teachers.

D. The interaction in class is not very good.

37. Which of the following is NOT included here as a way to improve fairness?

A. Having more people to decide on the final points.

B. Covering the names of the students in advance.

C. Getting students to do computer assisted tests.

D. Inviting people new to students to give points.

Questions 38-40

Most senior citizens in Taiwan are not willing to live in a nursing home, and therefore the demands for Southeast Asian caregivers have soared in recent years. These caregivers live with the elderly in most cases. In the beginning and perhaps throughout the whole stay, they face communication problems with the old people they look after and their employers. To many caregivers from Southeast Asia, the lack of respect is what bothers them most in the families they live with. People who hire these foreign caregivers sometimes ask them to do duties more than required, such as housework and grocery shopping. The employers should think twice before doing so because many such cases have been reported. On the other hand, too much workload affects the quality of care provided for the elderly. In the end, it is the loss of the employers.

38. What is the report mainly about?

A. Nursing homes for the elderly and their qualities in Taiwan.

B. Caregivers from Southeast Asia and their situations in Taiwan.

C. Agencies of foreign laborers and their operation in Taiwan.

D. Taiwanese children and Southeast Asian nannies.

39. According to this passage, why do we need so many foreign caregivers for the elderly in Taiwan?

A. The elderly do not want to move into an old people's home.

B. The elderly cannot afford the costs of a nursing home.

C. The elderly do not have good retirement plans.

D. The elderly want to have interaction with foreigners.

40. What annoys Southeast Asian caregivers most in the families they live with?

A. They do not have the right to take time off.

B. They do not have proper health insurances.

C. They feel they cannot communicate with them.

D. They feel they are not respected at all.

中級
新制全民英檢
Reading & Writing
NEW
GEPT
The General English Proficiency Test [Intermediate]

閱讀&寫作 模擬試題 +解答

GEPT 中級閱讀測驗
模擬試題第三回解答

1. C	11.	A	21.	C	31.	A
2. B	12.	B	22.	A	32.	B
3. C	13.	B	23.	D	33.	C
4. B	14.	C	24.	A	34.	B
5. D	15.	B	25.	B	35.	C
6. B	16.	B	26.	B	36.	A
7. A	17.	B	27.	B	37.	C
8. C	18.	A	28.	D	38.	B
9. C	19.	D	29.	B	39.	A
10.B	20.	B	30.	D	40.	D

第三回閱讀模擬試題解答與翻譯

英語能力分級檢定測驗中級
閱讀能力測驗

　　本測驗分三部份，全為四選一之選擇題，每部份各 15 題，共 45 題。本測驗總分 100 分，平均每題 2.2 分，作答時間 45 分鐘。

中級 Reading & Writing
NEW
新制全民英檢
GEPT
The General English Proficiency Test [Intermediate]
閱讀&寫作 模擬試題 +解答

第一部分：詞彙和結構

本部份共 15 題，每題有一個空格。請就試題冊上提供的 A、B、C、D 四個選項中選出最適合題意的字或詞，標示在答案紙上。

例：

After the police arrive, they will begin to interview the people who _____ in the jewelry store at the time of the robbery.

A. have been

B. will be

C. were

D. are

正確答案為 C，請在答案紙上塗黑作答。

1. _____ did you celebrate your last birthday?

A. Who

B. What

C. How

D. Which

你上個生日是 _____ 慶祝的？

A. 誰

B. 什麼

C. 如何

D. 關係代名詞

正確答案：C

☆解題關鍵

根據句意，此處符合文法的是選項 C：How（如何），因為如果要選 A，必須是 "With whom"；因為已經有 "your last birthday" 這個受詞，所以不能選 B：What；而選項 D：Which 前面應有名詞。

2. Mathmatics _____ his best subject in junior high school.

A. were

B. was

C. used to

D. are

數學 _____ 他在高中時最好的學科。

A. be 動詞的過去複數形式

B. be 動詞的過去單數形式

C. 過去曾經是

D. be 動詞的現在複數形式

正確答案：B

☆解題關鍵

根據句意，此處的意思是「過去曾經是」，"used to be" 和 "was" 都是正確答案，但是選項 C 少了 be 動詞，所以答案是選項 B。"mathmatics"（數學）雖然以 "s" 結尾，但是本身是一門學科，為一個單數名詞。

3. We all _____ mistakes in our lives, but the important thing is not to repeat the same mistakes.

A. do

B. done

C. make

D. take

我們都會 _____ 錯誤，但是最重要的是不要重複同樣錯誤。

A. do（做）的動詞原形

B. do（做）的過去分詞

C. make（做）的動詞原形

D. 拿

正確答案：C

☆解題關鍵

「犯錯」的固定片語是 "make a mistake"，複數為 "make mistakes"。

4. This is the place _____ I first met Ms. Lin seven years ago.

A. when

B. where

C. which

D. whose

這就是我七年前初次遇見林先生的地方。

A. 時間的關係副詞

B. 地方的關係副詞

C. 關係代名詞

D. 所有格關係代名詞，意思為「誰的；那人的，那些人的…」。

正確答案：B

☆解題關鍵

因為此處的關係代名詞緊接著 **"place"**，所以只能用地方的關係代名詞 **"where"**。

5. The appointment was _____ because of her illness, and she hasn't felt better since then.

A. put away

B. put down

C. put out

D. put off

這個約會因為她的病 _____ 了，從那時起，她的病情沒有好轉。

A. 收拾

B. 放下；安樂死

C. 熄滅

D. 順延

正確答案：D

☆解題關鍵

因為生病所以約會只有「順延」了，因此答案為選項 D：put off，順延。

6. Do you usually buy your lunch or cook the meal _____？

A. by your mother

B. by yourself

C. by day

D. by you

通常你會買午餐還是 _____ 做飯？

A. 靠你母親來做

B. 靠你自己來做

C. 白天

D. 靠你來做

正確答案：B

☆解題關鍵

標準答案為選項 B："by yourself"，意思是「靠你自己來做」，也可以只用 "yourself"，而 "by oneself" 較 "oneself" 更加強調是「靠某人自己的能力」完成的。

7. Like most friends of mine, I _____ Chinese dishes to western food.
A. prefer
B. enjoy
C. cook
D. prepare

就像我的大部分朋友一樣，比起西餐，我 _____ 中國料理。
A. 較喜歡
B. 享受
C. 烹飪
D. 準備

正確答案：A

☆解題關鍵

選項 A：prefer A to B 為常用片語，意思非常明顯，表示相較於 B，較喜歡 A。

8. ＿＿＿＿ do you think of the English final exam? Do you think it is too easy?
A. Which
B. When
C. What
D. Where

你認為英文期末考怎麼樣？你覺得太簡單了嗎？
A. 關係代名詞
B. 何時
C. 什麼
D. 何處

正確答案：C

☆解題關鍵

問某人對某事的意見要用 **"What do you think of something?"**。

9. _____ is the best policy. I think we should tell the truth.

A. Success

B. Happiness

C. Honesty

D. Diligence

_____ 為上策。我認為我們應該要說實話。

A. 成功

B. 幸福

C. 誠實

D. 勤奮

正確答案：C

☆解題關鍵

"Honesty is the best policy" 為一成語，意思是「誠實為上策」，

但是如果不知道這個片語，也可以由第二句中得知答案。

10. Yesterday I caught a serious cold, but now I already feel much
_____.
A. caring
B. better
C. generous
D. moved

昨天我重感冒，但是現在我已經感覺 _____ 多了。
A. 關心的
B. 較好的
C. 慷慨的
D. 感動的

正確答案：B

☆解題關鍵

因為前後用 **"but"** 來連接，所以前後的意思應該是相對的，因此
要選 B。

中級 Reading & Writing

新制全民英檢

GEPT

The General English Proficiency Test [Intermediate]

NEW

閱讀&寫作 模擬試題 +解答

11. He is _____ of the teacher's eye, but many fellow students do not like him.

A. apple

B. cake

C. sugar

D. sweets

他是老師 _____ 的學生，但是很多同學不喜歡他。

A. 蘋果

B. 蛋糕

C. 糖

D. 甜點

正確答案：A

☆解題關鍵

片語："apple of one's eye" 表示「極珍貴的東西」，也就是「極珍愛之人或物」。

12. He didn't sleep well last night, and _____, he failed the English test this morning.

A. in agreement with

B. as a result

C. according to

D. as far as

他昨晚沒睡好，_____ 他今早的英文考試不及格。

A. 與…相符合

B. 結果

C. 依照

D. 就…而言

正確答案：B

☆解題關鍵

因為前後有因果關係，所以答案只能選 B。

13. Yesterday I had _____ much homework to do that I couldn't work out in the gym.

A. as

B. so

C. yet

D. more

昨天我有 _____ 多功課以至於無法去健身中心運動。

A. 如同

B. 如此

C. 尚未

D. 更多

正確答案：B

☆解題關鍵

片語："so…that" 如此…以至於。前後必須有因果關係。

14. Most young people like to study in a coeducational high school, _____ I prefer not.

A. when

B. so

C. but

D. what

大部分年輕人喜歡讀男女合校的高中，_____ 我寧可不要。

A. 當

B. 所以

C. 但是

D. 什麼

正確答案：C

☆解題關鍵

因為這裡需要表示轉折語氣的連接詞，所以應該要用 "but"（但是）。

15. No matter _____ you say, she will not forgive you.

A. when

B. what

C. whatever

D. whenever

無論你説 _____，她都不會原諒你。

A. 當

B. 什麼

C. 無論什麼

D. 無論何時

正確答案：B

☆解題關鍵

「無論什麼」有兩種表達方式："no matter what" 和 "whatever"，但是不可混在一起使用，所以答案為選項 B：what。

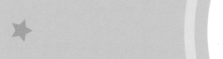

第二部分：段落填空

本部份共 15 題，包括二至三個段落，每個段落各含 5 個空格。請就試題冊上提供的 A、B、C、D 四個選項中選出最適合題意的字或詞，標示在答案紙上。

例：

Susan had a terrible day today. First she (1) up by a strange phone call at four o'clock this morning. When she was about to (2) the receiver, the phone stopped ringing. Then, she got up late and (3) the company bus, so she was thirty minutes late for work, (4) made her boss very angry. What was (5) , when she got home this afternoon, she couldn't open the door because she had left her keys at her office.

1. A. woke

   B. was woken

   C. wakes

   D. is awake

   (正確答案：B)

2. A. pick up

   B. pick

   C. pick at

中級 Reading & Writing
新制全民英檢
GEPT
The General English Proficiency Test [Intermediate]
NEW
閱讀&寫作 模擬試題 +解答

D. pick on

(正確答案：A)

3. A. dropped

   B. lost

   C. missed

   D. left

   (正確答案：C)

4. A. that

   B. this

   C. what

   D. which

   (正確答案：D)

5. A. harder

   B. worse

   C. later

   D. angrier

   (正確答案：B)

Questions 16-20

To most students in Taiwan, listening comprehension is the most difficult part of English tests. In fact, they can take (16) of media, such as radio broadcasting, TV news report and Internet resources, etc. In addition, they can listen to radio English learning programs. If they make an (17) to listen to English about 30 minutes a day, they can see great improvement. Some students (18) to watch movies in English to train their listening. The speed of dialogs in most movies is so fast that viewers have to (19) on the subtitles. In (20) to learn English effectively, most teachers recommend to use suitable matetials designed especially for learners.

中譯

對大多數的學生來說，聽力測驗是英語考試中最困難的部分。事實上，他們可以多善用媒體，像是電台廣播、電視新聞、網際網路等等。除此之外，他們可以聽英語廣播教學節目。如果他們每天努力聽約三十分鐘的英語，便可以看見非常大的進步。有些學生比較喜歡看英語電影來訓練聽力，大多電影中的對話速度快到觀眾必須要仰賴字幕。為了能有效學習英語，大多老師建議使用特別為學習者設計的合適教材。

16. A. care　照顧

　　B. advantage　善用

　　C. use　使用

　　D. time　時間

17. A. news　消息

　　B. effort　努力

　　C. work　工作

　　D. talent　天份

18. A. prefer　較喜歡

　　B. rather　較不喜歡

　　C. intend　想要

　　D. interest　感興趣

19. A. attend　出席

　　B. repeat　重覆

　　C. make　做

　　D. rely　仰賴

20. A. goal　目標

　　B. order　目的

　　C. purpose　意圖

D. achievement　成就

正確答案：16.(B)　17.(B)　18.(A)　19.(D)　20.(B)

➥重要字彙和片語

☆ take an advantage of 善用；利用

例：Nobody wants to be taken advantage of.

沒有人想要被利用。

☆ make an effort 努力

例：Now he really makes an effort to work out.

現在他真的很努力健身。

中級 Reading & Writing
新制全民英檢
GEPT
The General English Proficiency Test [Intermediate]
NEW

閱讀&寫作 模擬試題 +解答

Questions 21-25

The umployment rate in Taiwan has in recent years risen tremendously. As a result, many college graduates have to (21) up jobs which did not require a college degree in the past, such as factory workers, taxi drivers and so on. Some say it is a waste of educational resources; (22) think that at least these overqualified people are not out of work. People who are out of (23) tend to create many problems for the society, especially young people who enter the job market for the first time. During the time of unemployment, the unemployed are suggested to take new courses to learn new skills, like computer softwares, and keep in (24) with people in their trades. Quite often, the employers and colleagues in the past can introduce new jobs to the (25) .

中譯

台灣的失業率近幾年來極度攀升。結果很多大學畢業生必須要接受在從前不需要大學文憑的工作，像是工廠工人、計程車司機等等。有些人說這是教育資源的浪費；有些人則說至少這些資歷過高的人沒失業。失業的人傾向於製造很多社會問題，特別是首度進入就業市場的年輕人。在待業期間，一般建議失業者修習新課程來學新技能，像是電腦軟體，同時和業界的人保持聯絡。從前的雇主和同事經常能夠介紹新工作給求職者。

21. A. train　訓練

　　B. obtain　獲得

　　C. take　接受

　　D. get　得到

22. A. others　其他人

　　B. other　其他的

　　C. another　第三者的

　　D. those　那些

23. A. home　家庭

　　B. meaning　意義

　　C. assigment　任務

　　D. employment　職業

24. A. contact　聯絡

　　B. conclusion　結論

　　C. view　主張

　　D. control　控制

25. A. supervisors　主管
　　B. job-seekers　求職者
　　C. human resources　人力資源
　　D. outsourcing　外包

正確答案：21.(C)　22.(A)　23.(D)　24.(A)　25.(B)

➥重要字彙和片語

☆ out of employment/work 失業

例：Young people who are out of employment/work should look for jobs as soon as possible.

失業的年輕人要儘早找工作。

☆ Keep in contact with somebody 與某人保持聯絡

例：She keeps in contact with her high school friends.

她和高中朋友保持聯絡。

第三部分：閱讀理解

　　本部份共 15 題，包括數段短文，每段短文後有 2~5 個相關問題，試題冊上均提供 A、B、C、D 四個選項，請由四個選項中選出最適合者，標示在答案紙上。

　　例：

Scotland Yard first began to use dogs for police work in 1946. At that time, they used only four dogs. Today, more than 300 police dogs are working in London. When a young dog is three months old, it goes to the home of a policeman. This person will be the dog's "handler." The dog stays at its handler's home, lives with his family, and plays with the children. A handler must really know his dog.

1. How old is a dog when it goes to its handler's home?

A. Three months old.

B. Six months old.

C. Nine months old.

D. One year old.

（正確答案：A）

2. What is the article mainly about?

A. Policemen.

B. Police dogs.

C. Handlers.

D. Scotland Yard.

(正確答案：B)

Questions 26-28

More and more parents are concerned about the negative influences of violent computer games on their children. Of all the noticeable bad impacts of computer games, aggression is most worrying to parents and educational experts. It is no secret that gun shooting computer games are especially popular among boys and male teenagers. Many male students would rather spend hours of playing computer games than do any other things in their free time. An increasing number of male teenagers are so addicted to computer games that their daily lives are being interfered. Some parents still allow them to play computer games simply because they do not know how to deal with their kids if the computer games are taken away from them.

越來越多家長關心暴力電玩對他們孩子的負面影響。在所有電玩顯著的不良影響中，家長和教育專家認為侵略行為最讓人擔心。槍擊電玩特別受男孩和男性青少年喜歡，這一點並不是什麼秘密。很多男學生有空寧願花好幾小時打電玩，也不願做其他任何事。沈迷於電玩以至於日常生活受到干擾的男性青少年人數日益增多。有些家長仍讓這些人打電玩，因為如果將電腦撤開後，他們真的完全不知道如何處理孩子的反應。

26. What is the main idea of this passage?

A. Computer games and their designers.

B. Computer games and their negative influences.

C. Computer game industry and its future.

D. Computer games and the social media.

這篇文章的大意為何？

A. 電玩和電玩設計師

B. 電玩和電玩的負面影響

C. 電玩產業和電玩的未來

D. 電玩和社群媒體

27. What negative impact of computer games on children is

　　 most obvious?

211

NEW

中級 Reading & Writing
新制全民英檢
GEPT
The General English Proficiency Test [Intermediate]

閱讀&寫作 模擬試題 +解答

A. Positive thinking.

B. Aggressive behavior.

C. Improved social skills.

D. Outgoing personality.

電玩的什麼負面影響對孩童最為明顯？

A. 正面思考

B. 侵略行為

C. 進步的社交技巧

D. 活潑個性

28. Why do many parents still allow their children to play computer games?

A. Their children are the designers of the games.

B. Their children do not have other hobbies.

C. Their children show improvements in the games.

D. Their children are addicted to computer games.

為什麼很多家長仍讓他們的孩子打電玩？

A. 他們的小孩是電玩遊戲設計師

B. 他們的小孩沒有其他興趣

C. 他們的小孩在電玩遊戲方面進步很多

D. 他們的小孩沉迷於電玩遊戲

正確答案：26.(B) 27.(B) 28.(D)

Questions 29-31

　　Among Taiwanese university students, male and female students are about equal in numbers and in acheivements. Once they enter the job market, males dominate the leadership in almost all companies. Although many female employees think it is due to the unfair system of promotion, most leading women at the top level think it is women who stop themselves from going ahead. It is not uncommon to see female employees decline the chance of promotion because of family reasons. Males on the other hand seldom do the same. It shows clearly that many female employees do not think it is possible to have work family balance if they take up higher positions. Many women in the managerial roles encourage young female employees to be brave and to succeed in both career and in family.

　　台灣大學生當中，男學生和女學生的人數和成績相近，一旦進入

就業市場後,男性幾乎占據了所有公司的領導階層。雖然很多女性員工認為這是因為晉升系統不公平,但大部分高層的女性領導者認為是女性自己限制自己向上爬。女性員工因為家庭因素而婉拒升遷的情形並不少見,而男性卻很少會這樣做。這顯示很多女性員工認為一旦接受高階工作,可能無法保持工作和家庭的平衡。很多女性經理人鼓勵年輕女員工要勇敢追求職場和家庭的成功。

29. What is this passage mainly about?

A. Housework for men and women.

B. Women at the workplace.

C. Female staff in a university.

D. Female graduates in the job market.

這篇文章的大意為何?

A. 男性和女性的家事

B. 工作場所的女性

C. 大學的女性職員

D. 就業市場的女性大學畢業生

30. According to this passage, what stops most women from advancing in their careers?

A. The pressure from the decision-makers.

B. The males do not want female supervisors.

C. They do not have the motivation to succeed.

D. The limits they set for themselves.

根據這篇文章，什麼限制了女性在職場上的升遷？

A. 決策者的壓力

B. 男性不想要女性主管

C. 她們沒有成功的動力

D. 她們給自己所設的限制

31. What do many leading women want young female employees to do?

A. To believe they can have work family balance.

B. To go back to business schools to get MBA degrees.

C. To get to know more business contacts.

D. To focus on work and career development.

許多女性領導者希望年輕的女性員工怎樣做？

A. 相信自己可以保持工作和家庭的平衡

B. 回到商學院去修商管碩士學位

C. 結識更多商業人士

D. 專注於工作和職場規劃

正確答案：29.(B) 30.(D) 31.(A)

Questions 32-34

Since the middle of last December, many customers have been complaining about not receiving any products after they remitted the money to an online company. Many customers had collected all the money from their acquaintances in order to get special discounts. Now they lost not only their own money but also others'. The business owners have disappeared for the last couple of weeks, and until now there is no sign of showing up. It is estimated that they had collected more than one million Taiwan Dollars, and many customers believe it is an intended fraud. Quite a few consumer proection groups ask the customers to pay special attention to online shopping because such frauds are often not covered in our current laws.

自從去年十二月中旬以來，很多消費者抱怨匯錢給某家網購公司後沒有收到任何產品。不少消費者是從他們的熟人那邊集資來獲得折扣的，現在他們不但損失了他們自己的錢，也損失了別人的錢。負責人已經兩三個星期消失不見蹤影，至今沒有任何跡象會再出現。據估計他們所共獲得的錢超過一百萬台幣，而且很多消費者認為這是蓄意詐欺。很多消保團體要消費者特別小心網購，因為我們現行的法規經常沒有規範到這類的詐欺。

32. What is the topic of this report?

A. A case of privacy in the Internet.

B. A case of business fraud in the Internet.

C. A case of virtual dating in the Internet.

D. A case of tax fraud in the Internet.

這篇報導的主題為何？

A. 網路隱私的一個案例

B. 網購詐騙的一個案例

C. 網路交友的一個案例

D. 網路詐稅的一個案例

33. What does "others'" after "but also" mean here?

A. Other people's products.

B. Other people's reputation.

中級 Reading & Writing
新制全民英檢
GEPT
The General English Proficiency Test [Intermediate]
NEW
閱讀&寫作 模擬試題 +解答

C. Other people's money.

D. Other people's packages.

在 "but also" 後面的 "others'" 意思是？

A. 別人的產品

B. 別人的聲譽

C. 別人的金錢

D. 別人的包裝

34. Why do consumer proection groups ask the customers to pay special attention to online shopping?

A. Because of the prices of online products.

B. Because of the gray zone in online shopping

C. Because of the convenience of shopping.

D. Because of the privacy of online shoppings.

為什麼消保團體要消費者特別小心網購？

A. 因為網購產品的價格

B. 因為網購的灰色地帶

C. 因為網購的便利

D. 因為網購的隱私

正確答案：32.(B) 33.(C) 34.(B)

Questions 35-37

Fairness is what most students require of their teachers, but most teachers find it extremely hard to achieve. In fact, in the experiences of almost all teachers, absolute objectivity is nearly impossible. The interaction that teachers have with their students in class leaves them with particular impressions of the students. Although all teachers try their best to be objective, teachers might give points based on their previous opinions about the students. To solve this problem, more people might be included in grading entrance exams. Experts who haven't met the students are frequently invited to judge students' presentations. Quite often the names of students are covered in order to help teachers remain objective in grading the papers.

大部分學生要求老師要公平，但是大部分老師覺得要做到這一點非常困難。事實上，在大多數老師的經驗中，完全客觀幾乎是不可能的。老師在課堂上和學生的互動會留給老師對學生特別的印象。雖然

所有老師都盡可能試圖做到客觀，但是老師還是可能會根據他們之前對學生的看法來評分。為了解決這個問題，可能會要多一點人來共同批改入學考試的考卷。沒有見過學生的專家經常受邀作為學生成果發表會的評審。學生的名字經常會被遮起來以便老師在改論文時保持客觀。

35. What is the main topic of this passage?

A. Fair trading does not exist at all.

B. Objective grading is very common.

C. Teachers are not likely to be totally fair.

D. Students interfere with teachers' privacy.

這篇文章的主旨為何？

A. 公平交易根本不存在

B. 客觀的評分很常見

C. 老師不太可能完全公平

D. 學生干擾老師的隱私權

36. According to this passage, why is it not easy for teachers to be completely fair and objective?

A. Most teachers have their opinions about their students.

B. Teachers do not know their students at all.

C. Most students do not respect their teachers.

D. The interaction in class is not very good.

根據這篇文章，為什麼要老師完全公平客觀並不容易？

A. 大部分老師對學生有他們的看法

B. 老師一點也不認識他們的學生

C. 大部分學生不尊敬他們的老師

D. 課堂上的互動欠佳

37. Which of the following is NOT included here as a way to improve fairness?

A. Having more people to decide on the final points.

B. Covering the names of the students in advance.

C. Getting students to take computer assisted tests.

D. Inviting people new to students to give points.

下列哪一點不是這裡用來改善公平性的方法？

A. 多請些人來決定最終成績

B. 事先將學生名字遮起來

C. 要求學生用電腦考試

D. 請不認識學生的人來評分

正確答案：35.(C) 36.(A) 37.(C)

Questions 38-40

Most senior citizens in Taiwan are not willing to live in a nursing home, and therefore the demands for Southeast Asian care-takers have soared in recent years. These care-takers live with the elderly in most cases. In the beginning and perhaps throughout the whole stay, they face communication problems with the old people they look after and their employers. To many care-takers from Southeast Asia, the lack of respect is what bothers them most in the families they live with. People who hire these foreign care-takers sometimes ask them to do duties more than required, such as housework and grocery shopping. The employers should think twice before doing so because many such cases have been reported. On the other hand, too much workload affects the quality of care provided for the elderly. In the end, it is the loss of the employers.

大多數的台灣銀髮族不願意住在老人養護中心，因此近年來對東南亞看護的需求快速攀升。通常這些看護和長者住在一起。在剛開始時，或許在全部停留時間內，他們面臨和所照顧的長者還有和雇主的溝通障礙。對很多東南亞看護來說，缺乏尊敬為他們住在這些家庭裡最感到困擾的一點。雇用這些外籍看護的人有時要求他們負責過多的任務，像是做家事和購物。想要這麼做的雇主可要好好考慮了，因為已經有很多這樣的案例被檢舉了。就另一方面來說，過多的工作量會影響老人的看護品質，最後損失的還是雇主。

38. What is the report mainly about?

A. Nursing homes for the elderly and their qualities in Taiwan.

B. Care-takers from Southeast Asia and their situations in Taiwan.

C. Agencies of foreign laborers and their operation in Taiwan.

D. Taiwanese children and Southeast Asian nannies.

這篇報導主要的內容是關於？

A. 台灣銀髮族的看護中心與其品質

B. 東南亞看護和他們在台灣的處境

C. 外籍勞工仲介所和他們在台灣的運作

D. 台灣小孩和東南亞保姆

39. According to this passage, why do we need so many foreign care-

中級 Reading & Writing

NEW

新制全民英檢

GEPT

The General English Proficiency Test [Intermediate]

閱讀&寫作 模擬試題 +解答

takers for the elderly in Taiwan?

A. The elderly do not want to move into an old people's home.

B. The elderly cannot afford the costs of a nursing home.

C. The elderly do not have good retirement plans.

D. The elderly want to have interaction with foreigners.

根據這篇文章，為什麼台灣需要這麼多的老人外籍看護？

A. 長者不願搬進老人安養中心

B. 長者無法負擔老人安養中心的費用

C. 長者沒有很好的退休計劃

D. 長者想要和外國人互動

40. What annoys Southeast Asian care-takers most in the families

they live with?

A. They do not have the right to take time off.

B. They do not have proper health insurances.

C. They feel they cannot communicate with them.

D. They feel they are not respected at all.

在這些家庭裡最令東南亞看護感到困擾的一點是什麼？

A. 他們沒有請假的權利

B. 他們沒有完整的健康保險

C. 他們覺得無法和他們溝通

D. 他們覺得他們完全不受到尊重

正確答案：38.(B) 39.(A) 40.(D)

中級 Reading & Writing

NEW

新制全民英檢
GEPT

The General English Proficiency Test [Intermediate]

閱讀&寫作 模擬試題
+解答

寫作模擬試題

※ 本章共包含三回寫作模擬試題

中級 Reading & Writing

新制全民英檢

GEPT

The General English Proficiency Test [Intermediate]

閱讀&寫作 模擬試題 +解答

第一回寫作模擬試題

本測驗共分中譯英及英文作文兩部分，測驗時間為 40 分鐘。

一、中譯英 (40 分)

説明 : 請將下列的一段中文翻譯成通順、達意且前後連貫的英文。答案請寫在「寫作能力測驗答案紙」標示的位置上。

許多人沒有規律運動的習慣。直到他們生病了才知道健康的重要。規律運動可以避免疾病的發生。選擇自己有興趣的運動，並且結交運動夥伴，都可以幫助自己不要中途而廢。找到適合自己的運動團體，對自己幫助最大。

二、英文作文 (60 分)

説明：請依下面所提供的圖片及文字提示寫一篇英文作文，長度約一百二十字 (8 至 12 個句子)。

作文可以是一個完整的段落，也可以分成兩段，請書寫在「寫作能力測驗答案紙」標示的位置上。評分重點包括內容、組織、文法、用字遣詞、標點符號、大小寫。

提示：

　　每個人都需要朋友，但是並不是所有人都知道如何交朋友。請談談你認為交朋友的一些好方法，還有哪些事和朋友往來時該避免的？

第一回寫作模擬試題
參考解答

Track **17**

一、中譯英 (40 分)

許多人沒有規律運動的習慣。直到他們生病了才知道健康的重要。規律運動可以預防疾病。選擇自己有興趣的運動,並且結交運動夥伴,都可以幫助自己不要中途而廢。找到適合自己的運動團體,幫助最大。

Many people do not have the habit of regular exercise. It is not until they get sick that they understand the importance of health. Regular exercise can prevent illnesses. Choosing a sport that you are interested in and making friends with sports partners can help you not give up exercising. It helps most if you find a sports group that suits you.

Track **18**

二、英文作文 (60 分)(說明與提示請見模擬試題)

No man is an island, and nobody can live without friends. Good

230

friends can offer advice to us because they know us well. When we are in need, we can always rely on true friends for help. If we always put ourselves in the shoes of our friends, we will know what to do for them. One mistake many people make is not caring about their friends enough. We should listen to our friends and not just be interested in talking about ourselves. Giving a hand to your friends is, of course, much more important than talking. It is necessary to frequently check what is working and what is not working with your friends. In this way, we can know what can work better with each different friend.

中譯

　　沒有人是孤島，沒有人可以沒有朋友。好朋友可以提供我們建議，因為他們對我們很了解。我們有需要的時候，總是可以仰賴真正的朋友來幫助我們。如果我們總是站在朋友的立場上，我們就會知道該為他們做些什麼。很多人犯的錯誤是不夠關心他們的朋友。我們應該要聆聽朋友的傾訴，而不是只對談論我們自己的事感興趣。當然，比起光說更重要的是對你的朋友伸出援手。我們要經常檢查和朋友之間什麼是行得通的，什麼是行不通的。這樣一來，我們便能知道和每位不同的朋友要怎樣相處才會更好。

中級 Reading & Writing
新制全民英檢
GEPT
The General English Proficiency Test [Intermediate]
NEW

閱讀&寫作 模擬試題 +解答

第二回寫作模擬試題

本測驗共分中譯英及英文作文兩部分，測驗時間為 40 分鐘。

一、中譯英 (40 分)

説明：請將下列的一段中文翻譯成通順、達意且前後連貫的英文。答案請寫在「寫作能力測驗答案紙」標示的位置上。

昨天我在過馬路時，看到一個機車騎士，一邊騎機車，一邊在看手機。他差一點撞上了一個老太太。還好沒有任何意外發生。我認為開車或騎車的人應該注意專心，才不會造成自己和他人的危險。

二、英文作文 (60 分)

説明：請依下面所提供的圖片及文字提示寫一篇英文作文，長度約一百二十字 (8 至 12 個句子)。

作文可以是一個完整的段落，也可以分成兩段，請書寫在「寫作能力測驗答案紙」標示的位置上。評分重點包括內容、組織、文法、用字遣詞、標點符號、大小寫。

第五章
寫作模擬試題

提示：

1. 上個暑假，麗玲的父母帶她到住在美國的阿姨家住了兩個星期，受到了熱情的招待，尤其是阿姨的女兒麗莎，雖然只會說英語不太會說中文，也全程參與接待。現在，請你以麗玲的身份擬一封信給阿姨的女兒麗莎，謝謝他們全家的款待，並且邀請麗莎全家隨時來台灣玩。

2. 信的上下款應依下列方式寫出。

Feb. 21, 2014

Dear Lisa,

_____

_____

_____

_____

.

.

中級 Reading & Writing
新制全民英檢
GEPT
The General English Proficiency Test [Intermediate]
NEW
閱讀&寫作 模擬試題 +解答

.

_____

_____

_____

_____

Sincerely,

Liling

第二回寫作模擬試題
參考解答

一、中譯英 (40 分)

昨天我在過馬路時,看到一個機車騎士,一邊騎機車,一邊在看手機。他差一點撞上了一個老太太。還好沒有任何意外發生。我認為開車或騎車的人應該注意專心,才不會造成自己和他人的危險。

Yesterday when I was walking across the road, I saw a motorcycle driver, who was riding the motorcycle and reading his cellular phone at the same time. He almost ran into an old woman. Luckily no accident happened. I think drivers of cars or motorcycles should focus their mind so that they would not harm themselves and others.

Track**19**

二、英文作文 (60 分) (說明與提示請見模擬試題)

Feb. 21, 2014

Track20

Dear Lisa,

Thank you and your family very much for your hospitality during our 2-week stay in the States. We got along very well even though my English is not fluent and you do not speak much Chinese. Your mother drove us around almost every day for sightseeing. All the people in your community were very friendly to us. I especially enjoyed visiting your high school with you. For the first time in my life, I saw snow with my own eyes in your back yard.

If you have the chance to visit Taiwan, please let me be your travel guide. How about this coming summer? During summer vacation, we can do many activites here together.

Sincerely,
Liling

第五章
寫作模擬試題

中譯

2014 年 2 月 21 日

麗莎：

　　謝謝妳和妳家人在我們待在美國兩星期間的招待。雖然我的英文不流利，妳會的中文不多，但是我們相處非常融洽。妳母親幾乎每天開車載我們觀光。你們社區所有的人對我們都非常友善。我特別喜歡和妳一起去參觀妳的高中。在妳家後院，我生平第一次親眼看到雪。

　　如果妳有機會來台灣，請讓我作妳的導遊。妳看這個即將到來的夏天怎麼樣？在暑假中，我們可以一起在這裡做很多活動。

　　麗玲上

中級 Reading & Writing
新制全民英檢
GEPT
The General English Proficiency Test [Intermediate]

NEW

閱讀&寫作 模擬試題 +解答

第三回寫作模擬試題

本測驗共分中譯英及英文作文兩部分，測驗時間為 40 分鐘。

一、中譯英 (40 分)

說明：請將下列的一段中文翻譯成通順、達意且前後連貫的英文。答案請寫在「寫作能力測驗答案紙」標示的位置上。

很多人都知道閱讀的好處很多，但是並非所有人都喜歡閱讀英文文章。多讀英文報章雜誌可以學會很多有用的字彙，會話和寫作時都可以用到。閱讀不但可以增加新知，也可以學到別人的寫作技巧。

二、英文作文 (60 分)

說明：請依下面所提供的圖片及文字提示寫一篇英文作文，長度約一百二十字 (8 至 12 個句子)。

作文可以是一個完整的段落，也可以分成兩段，請書寫在「寫作能力測驗答案紙」標示的位置上。評分重點包括內容、組織、文法、用字遣詞、標點符號、大小寫。

第五章
寫作模擬試題

提示：

　　很多人都有想要寫書的念頭，如果你能夠出版任何一本你想要寫的書，你會針對什麼樣的主題來寫作？為什麼？

中級 Reading & Writing
新制全民英檢
GEPT
The General English Proficiency Test [Intermediate]
NEW
閱讀&寫作 模擬試題+解答

第三回寫作模擬試題 參考解答

Track**21**

一、中譯英 (40 分)

很多人都知道閱讀的好處很多,但是並非所有人都喜歡閱讀英文文章。多讀英文報章雜誌可以學會很多有用的字彙,會話和寫作時都可以用到。閱讀不但可以增加新知,也可以學到別人的寫作技巧。

Many people know how good reading can be, but not all people like reading English articles. When you read many English newspapers and magazines, you can learn a lot of useful vocabulary, which can be used in conversation and in writing. Through reading, you can not only gain new knowledge but also learn writing skills from others.

Track**22**

二、英文作文 (60 分)(說明與提示請見模擬試題)

If I can write a book of my own, I would like to write about caring

for the people with mental and physical disabilities. We can see some shops selling products made by the people with disabilities, such as biscuits. These caring business operations can help their employees with their financial problems. Many workers with disabilities can learn and grow with suitable work opportunities. Providing these unfortunate people with good working relationships can give them self-respect, and people around these workers with disabilities will respect them, too. Generally speaking, the lack of respect for the people with disabilities is serious in our society. This is why I would like to write a book to talk about these issues.

中譯

　　如果我能寫一本書，我想要寫關於照顧身心障礙人士的議題。我們可以看到一些商店在賣這些身心障礙者所做的產品，像是愛心餅乾，這些公益企業可以幫助他們的員工解決財務問題。很多身心障礙員工可以因為合適的工作機會而學習、成長。提供良好的工作關係給這些不幸的人可以帶給他們自尊，這些身心障礙工作者周圍的人也會尊敬他們。普遍而言，我們社會嚴重缺乏對身心障礙人士的尊重，這就是我為什麼想要寫本書來探討這些議題的原因。

中級 Reading & Writing

NEW

新制全民英檢
GEPT

The General English Proficiency Test [Intermediate]

閱讀&寫作 模擬試題 +解答

CHAPTER

6

520 個最常考的中級字彙

中級 Reading & Writing
新制全民英檢
GEPT
The General English Proficiency Test [Intermediate]
NEW
閱讀&寫作 模擬試題 +解答

Track**23**

A

absence　　n.　缺席，缺乏

【同義詞】

nonattendance, nonresidence, nonappearance, unavailability

absolute　　a.　純粹的；完全的

【同義詞】

complete, perfect, thorough, total

absorb　　v.　吸收

【同義詞】

incorporate, sponge, assimilate

abuse　　v.　虐待；濫用

【同義詞】

injure, damage, mistreat, maltreat

academic　　a.　大學的；學術的

【同義詞】

educational, learned, scholarly

acceptable　　a.　可以接受的；值得接受的

【同義詞】

worthy, deserving, competent

access　　n.　接近，進入；接近的機會或權利

【同義詞】

admission, entrance, entry

accommodation　　n.　住處；適應

【同義詞】

housing, lodging, residence; adaptation, adjustmet, compromise

Track**23**

accompany　　v.　陪同，伴隨

【同義詞】

escort, join, come along

accomplish　　v.　完成，實現，達到

【同義詞】

realize, do, complete, perform

accountant　　n.　會計師；會計人員

【同義詞】

bookkeeper, auditor, controller

accuracy　　n.　正確（性）；準確（性）

【同義詞】

accurateness, exactness, exactitude, precision

ache　　v.　疼痛

【同義詞】

hurt, suffer

achievement　　n.　達成；完成

【同義詞】

accomplishment, feat, deed, act

中級 Reading & Writing
新制全民英檢
GEPT
The General English Proficiency Test [Intermediate]

NEW

閱讀&寫作 模擬試題+解答

Track**24**

acquaintance   n.   相識的人，熟人

【同義詞】

colleague, associate, peer, teammate

adapt   v.   使適應，使適合

【同義詞】

modify, adjust, alter, vary

additional   a.   添加的；附加的；額外的

【同義詞】

supplementary, supplemental, extra

adequate   a.   足夠的

【同義詞】

satisfactory, sufficient, enough, plenty

adjust   v.   調節；改變 . . . 以適應

【同義詞】

alter, vary, arrange, change

administration   n.   管理，經營；監督

【同義詞】

direction, management, organization, supervision

admiration   n.   欽佩，讚美，羨慕

【同義詞】

appreciation, approval, compliment, esteem, praise, respect

admission   n.   進入許可

Track**24**

【同義詞】

fee, cost, charge, bill

| **advanced** | a. | 在前面的；高級的 |

【同義詞】

forward, improved, bettered, developed

| **adventure** | n. | 冒險，冒險精神 |

【同義詞】

venture, take chances

| **advertise** | v. | 廣告；宣傳 |

【同義詞】

announce, notify, promote, publicize

| **adviser** | n. | 顧問；勸告者 |

【同義詞】

counsellor, guidance counsellor, mentor, confidant

| **affect** | v. | 影響；對 . . . 發生作用 |

【同義詞】

influence, sway, move, touch

| **afford** | v. | 買得起；有足夠的 . . . |

【同義詞】

have the means, offer, furnish, supply

| **afterward** | adv. | 之後，以後，後來 |

【同義詞】

中級 Reading & Writing
新制全民英檢
GEPT
The General English Proficiency Test [Intermediate]
NEW
閱讀&寫作 模擬試題 +解答

subsequently, after, then, next

agency n. 代辦處，經銷處，代理機構

【同義詞】

operation, office, work, management

aggressive a. 侵略的，侵犯的

【同義詞】

combative, offensive, hostile

agreement n. 同意，一致

【同義詞】

bargain, contract, pact, alliance

Track **25**

alcohol n. 酒精

【同義詞】

liquor, spirits

alley n. 小巷，胡同；後街

【同義詞】

passageway, opening

allowance n. 津貼，補貼；零用錢

【同義詞】

allotment, portion, grant, fee

altitude n. 高度；高處，高地

【同義詞】

height

ambassador　　　n.　大使；使節

【同義詞】

diplomat, attache, envoy

Track**25**

ambition　　n.　雄心，抱負

【同義詞】

aspiration, hoping, wishfulness, desire

amusement　　　n.　樂趣；興味

【同義詞】

entertainment, delight, pleasure, fun

analysis　　n.　分析；分解；解析

【同義詞】

examination, investigation, review

ancestor　　n.　祖宗，祖先

【同義詞】

forefather, forbear

angle　　n.　角；角度

【同義詞】

perspective, position, standpoint, viewpoint

anniversary　　　n.　週年紀念；週年紀念日

【同義詞】

birthday, centenary

announce　　　v.　宣佈，發佈

中級 Reading & Writing

NEW

新制全民英檢

GEPT

The General English Proficiency Test [Intermediate]

閱讀&寫作 模擬試題 +解答

【同義詞】

proclaim, broadcast, report, state

annoy v. 惹惱，使生氣

【同義詞】

tease, disturb, irritate

annual a. 一年的；一年一次的

【同義詞】

yearly, anniversary

anxiety n. 焦慮，掛念

【同義詞】

uneasiness

apology n. 道歉；陪罪

【同義詞】

excuse, justification

apparent a. 表面的，外觀的；未必真實的

【同義詞】

plain, clear, seeming, obvious

appeal v. 呼籲，懇求

【同義詞】

entreat, implore, plead, beg

appetite n. 食慾，胃口

【同義詞】

Track**26**

hunger, desire, craving

application　　　n.　應用，適用；運用

【同義詞】

use, utilization, employment, attention

appointment　　　n.　約會

【同義詞】

date, get-together, meeting

appreciation　　　n.　欣賞，鑑賞；賞識

【同義詞】

esteem, respect, taste, understanding

approach　　　n.　接近，靠近

【同義詞】

advance, entrance

appropriate　　　a.　適當的，恰當的，相稱的

【同義詞】

suitable, becoming, fitting, proper

approve　　v.　贊成，同意；贊許

【同義詞】

endorse, ratify, sanction, accredit

architecture　　　n.　建築學；建築術

【同義詞】

structure, construction, building

中級 Reading & Writing
新制全民英檢
GEPT
The General English Proficiency Test [Intermediate]
NEW
閱讀&寫作 模擬試題 +解答

argument　　　　n.　爭吵；辯論

【同義詞】

debate, disagreement, dispute

arrangement　　　n.　安排；準備工作

【同義詞】

order, organization, system, classification

arrow　　n.　箭

【同義詞】

shaft, bolt

artificial　　a.　人工的，人造的；假的

【同義詞】

false, pretended, unreal, substitute

artistic　　a.　藝術的；美術的；唯美（主義）的

【同義詞】

attractive, lovely, handsome, masterly

assignment　　　　n.　（分派的）任務；工作

Track**27**

【同義詞】

duty, responsibility, task

assistance　　　　n.　援助，幫助

【同義詞】

help, aid, avail, service

association　　　　n.　協會，公會，社團

【同義詞】

alliance, body, club, company

athlete　　n.　運動員，體育家

Track**27**

【同義詞】

sportsman, player

atmosphere　　n.　氣氛

【同義詞】

environment, feeling, mood, vibes

attachment　　n.　連接；安裝；附件

【同義詞】

accessory, addition, supplement

attempt　　v.　試圖；企圖；試圖做

【同義詞】

try, endeavor, undertake, strive

attitude　　n.　態度，意見，看法

【同義詞】

viewpoint, standpoint, position, opinion

attract　　v.　吸引

【同義詞】

tempt, charm, allure, fascinate

author　　n.　作者；作家

【同義詞】

中級 Reading & Writing

新制全民英檢

GEPT
The General English Proficiency Test [Intermediate]

NEW

閱讀&寫作 模擬試題+解答

writer, composer, scribbler, penman

average n. 一般，普通；中等

【同義詞】

usual, common, ordinary, general

awake v. 清醒的；意識到的

【同義詞】

active, conscious, alert, wakeful

award n. 獎，獎品；獎狀

【同義詞】

reward, prize, medal, trophy

awful a. 可怕的，嚇人的

【同義詞】

brutal, ruthless, terrible, horrible

awkward a. 笨拙的；不熟練的，不靈巧的

【同義詞】

clumsy, cumbersome, ungraceful

Track**28** **B**

babysit n. 當臨時保姆

【同義詞】

care for a child

Track 28

background　　n.　背景；出身背景，學經歷

【同義詞】

practice, knowledge, training, experience

backup　　n.　備用，備用物；後援，支持

【同義詞】

fill-in, relief, reserve, stand-in, substitute

backward　　a.　adv.　向後的，反向的，返回的

【同義詞】

rearward, in reverse, retrogressively, reversed

baggage　　n.　行李

【同義詞】

luggage, packages, pack, bags

balance　　n.　平衡，均衡

【同義詞】

harmony, level, match

balcony　　n.　陽臺，露臺

【同義詞】

porch, veranda, terrace, deck

bald　　a.　禿頭的，禿頂的

【同義詞】

open, uncovered, hairless, simple

balloon　　v.　像氣球般鼓起（或膨脹）

【同義詞】

inflate, swell, swell out

ban	v.	禁止；禁令

【同義詞】

bar, disallow, forbid, inhibit, outlaw, prohibit

bandage	v.	用繃帶包紮

【同義詞】

dress, compress

bankrupt	a.	破產的；有關破產的

【同義詞】

broke, destitute, impoverished, insolvent, poor

bare	a.	裸的

【同義詞】

naked, open, nude, bald

bargain	n.	協議；買賣，交易；便宜貨

【同義詞】

agreement, barter, deal, sale, transaction

bathe	v.	把...浸入，浸洗

【同義詞】

swim, launder, rinse, cover

bat	v.	用球棒或球拍打球

【同義詞】

Track**29**

knock, strike, hit

battle n. 戰鬥；戰役

Track**29**

【同義詞】

contest, conflict, struggle, fight

bay n. （海或湖泊的）灣

【同義詞】

harbour, cove, gulf

beast n. 獸，野獸

【同義詞】

animal, creature

beauty n. 美，美麗，優美

【同義詞】

loveliness, comeliness, fairness, prettiness

beg v. 乞討

【同義詞】

appeal, beseech, plead, implore

behavior n. 行為，舉止；態度

【同義詞】

conduct, action, deportment, acts

belly n. 腹部；肚子

【同義詞】

abdomen, stomach, paunch

中級 Reading & Writing
新制全民英檢
GEPT
The General English Proficiency Test [Intermediate]
NEW

閱讀&寫作 模擬試題 +解答

Track **29**

| **bend** | v. 使彎曲，折彎 |

【同義詞】

curve, turn, bow, stoop

| **beneath** | prep. ... 之下；（地位等）低於，劣於 |

【同義詞】

below, under

| **biscuit** | n. 小麵包；軟餅 |

【同義詞】

cookie, cooky

| **bleed** | v. 出血，流血 |

【同義詞】

drain, exhaust, grieve, pity

| **bless** | v. 為 ... 祝福，為 ... 祈神賜福 |

【同義詞】

praise, glorify, thank

| **blossom** | v. 開花 |

【同義詞】

develop, flower, bloom

| **blush** | v. 臉紅 |

【同義詞】

redden, colour, flush, crimson

| **boast** | v. 自吹自擂；誇耀 |

【同義詞】

brag, show off

| **bold** | | a. | 英勇的，無畏的；大膽的 |

【同義詞】

defiant, impudent, brazen, arrogant

| **bookshelf** | | n. | 書架；書櫃 |

【同義詞】

bookcase

| **bookstore** | | n. | 書店 |

【同義詞】

bookshop, bookstall

| **bow** | | v. | 鞠躬，欠身 |

【同義詞】

stoop, bend, kneel

| **brand** | | n. | 商標；牌子 |

【同義詞】

mark, label, burn, tag

| **bravery** | | n. | 勇敢，勇氣 |

【同義詞】

courage, gallantry, boldness, daring

| **breast** | | n. | 乳房 |

【同義詞】

中級 Reading & Writing
新制全民英檢
GEPT
The General English Proficiency Test [Intermediate]
NEW
閱讀&寫作 模擬試題+解答

Track**30**

chest, bosom, front

| **breathe** | v. | 呼吸；呼氣；吸氣 |

【同義詞】

respire, puff, pant, wheeze

| **briefcase** | n. | 公事包 |

【同義詞】

attache case

| **brilliant** | a. | 光輝的，明亮的；傑出的，出色的 |

【同義詞】

sparkling, bright, shining, clear

| **bubble** | n. | 水泡，氣泡，泡 |

【同義詞】

glob, drop, droplet

| **budget** | n. | 預算；預算費；生活費，經費 |

【同義詞】

ration, allowance, schedule

| **bulletin** | n. | 公報；公告 |

【同義詞】

message, circular, news, statement

| **bump** | v. | 碰，撞 |

【同義詞】

hit, shake, push, collide

bunch   n.   串，束

【同義詞】

cluster, group, set, batch

burger   n.   漢堡

【同義詞】

hamburger

C

Track**31**

cabin   n.   客艙

【同義詞】

hut, cottage, bungalow, house

calculate   v.   計算

【同義詞】

count, figure, compute, estimate

camping   n.   去露營

【同義詞】

tenting

candidate   n.   候選人；候補者

【同義詞】

seeker, nominee, applicant

capable   a.   有 ... 的能力

Track**31**

【同義詞】

intelligent, apt, smart, clever

cape	a.	披肩；斗篷

【同義詞】

cloak, mantle

cashier	n.	出納，出納員

【同義詞】

teller, banker, cambist, treasurer

casual	a.	偶然的，碰巧的

【同義詞】

accidental, chance, unexpected

catalog	n.	目錄；目錄冊，目錄簿

【同義詞】

list, classify, record, group

cattle	n.	牛

【同義詞】

livestock, stock, cows

cave	n.	洞穴，洞窟

【同義詞】

lair, shelter, den, cavern

celebration	n.	慶祝

【同義詞】

feast, festivity, party

| **certificate** | n. | 證明書；執照；結業證書 |

【同義詞】

document, testimonial, certification, documentation

| **chain** | n. | 鏈，鏈條；項圈 |

【同義詞】

band, bind, bond

| **challenge** | n. | 挑戰 |

【同義詞】

competition, contest

| **champion** | n. | 優勝者，冠軍 |

【同義詞】

winner, victor, choice, best

Track**32**

| **charity** | n. | 慈悲，仁愛，博愛；慈善 |

【同義詞】

generosity, liberality, liberalness

| **charm** | n. | 魅力 |

【同義詞】

attractiveness, appeal, allure, allurement

| **chat** | v. | 閒談，聊天 |

【同義詞】

gossip, talk, converse

Track **32**

check	n.	檢查，檢驗，核對

【同義詞】

stop, control, restrain, curb

cheek	n.	臉頰；腮幫子

【同義詞】

jaw

cheerful	a.	興高采烈的；情緒好的

【同義詞】

cheery, gay, sunny

chemist	n.	化學家；藥劑師，藥商

【同義詞】

druggist, pharmacist

cherish	v.	珍愛；撫育；愛護

【同義詞】

adore, worship, treasure, protect

chess	n.	西洋棋

【同義詞】

chess game

chest	n.	胸，胸膛；箱子，盒子

【同義詞】

box, locker, dresser, safe

chew	v.	嚼，咀嚼，嚼碎

【同義詞】

bite, grind, munch, nibble

chore	n.	家庭雜務；農莊雜務

【同義詞】

task, job, work, duty

chorus	n.	合唱隊

【同義詞】

choir, group, unison

cigarette	n.	香煙，紙煙，煙卷

【同義詞】

smoke, butt, cig, weed

cinema	n.	電影院

【同義詞】

motion picture, cine, film, movie

circular	a.	圓的，圓形的；環形的

【同義詞】

round, annular, ring-shaped

Track**33**

circus	n.	馬戲團；馬戲表演

【同義詞】

big top, carnival, rodeo, troupe

clinic	n.	診所，門診所

【同義詞】

Track**33**

infirmary, hospital, medical center

clown	n.	小丑，丑角

【同義詞】

fool, play, comic, performer

clue	n.	線索，跡象，提示

【同義詞】

hint, evidence, proof, sign

clumsy	a.	笨拙的，手腳不靈活的

【同義詞】

awkward, ungraceful, ungainly, cumbersome

code	n.	法典，法規；代碼，密碼

【同義詞】

laws, rules, system, signal

coincidence	n.	巧合；巧事；同時發生

【同義詞】

correspondence, identity, similarity

collar	n.	衣領

【同義詞】

neckband

colleague	n.	聯合；加盟

【同義詞】

co-worker, collaborator, fellow-worker

comfort　　v.　安慰，慰問

【同義詞】

console, ease, assure, relieve

commerce　　n.　商業，貿易，交易

【同義詞】

trade, business, dealings

communication　　n.　傳達；通信；傳染

【同義詞】

message, notice, report, statement

companion　　n.　同伴，伴侶；朋友

【同義詞】

partner, accompanist, buddy, friend

comparison　　n.　比較，對照；類似

【同義詞】

contrast, collation, confronting, likening

competition　　n.　競爭，角逐

【同義詞】

contest, game, match, tournament

comprehension　　n.　理解；理解力

Track**34**

【同義詞】

understanding, apprehension, intelligence, grasp

concentration　　n.　集中

Track**34**

【同義詞】

clustering, collection, massing

| **concept** | n. | 概念，觀念，思想 |

【同義詞】

thought, notion, idea, opinion

| **concert** | n. | 音樂會，演奏會 |

【同義詞】

music, recital

| **condition** | n. | 情況；（健康等）狀態 |

【同義詞】

provision, specification, state, circumstance

| **conduct** | v. | 引導，帶領 |

【同義詞】

manage, direct, guide, lead

| **conference** | n. | 會議；討論會，協商會 |

【同義詞】

meeting, convention, council, caucus

| **confidence** | n. | 自信，信心，把握 |

【同義詞】

trust, faith, reliance, dependence

| **congratulate** | v. | 祝賀；恭禧 |

【同義詞】

Track**34**

bless, compliment, flatter, commend

connect v. 連接，連結

【同義詞】

join, unite, combine, link

consideration n. 考慮

【同義詞】

attention, notice, advertency, examination

consult v. 與...商量

【同義詞】

confer, discuss, talk over

consumer n. 消費者；消耗者

【同義詞】

user, buyer, purchaser, shopper

coward n. 懦夫，膽怯者

【同義詞】

weakling

crash v. 碰撞，倒下，墜落

【同義詞】

strike, shatter, break, smash

credit n. 信譽；信用，榮譽；功勞

【同義詞】

belief, trust, faith, honor

Track **35**

creep	v.	躡手躡足地走；緩慢地行進

【同義詞】

crawl

criticize	v.	批評；批判；苛求；非難

【同義詞】

judge, appraise, assess

crown	n.	王冠；王位

【同義詞】

cap, peak, summit, tip, top

cue	n.	提示，尾白

【同義詞】

clue, hint, indication, sign, signal

curly	a.	蜷曲的；蜷縮的

【同義詞】

wavy, curled, kinky, frizzy

cyclist	n.	騎腳踏車的人

【同義詞】

biker, bicyclist

D

dairy	n.	乳品店；牛奶及乳品業

【同義詞】

creamery, dairy factory, dairy farm

| **damp** | a. | 有濕氣的；潮濕的 |

Track **35**

【同義詞】

moist, wettish, watery, dank

| **dare** | v. | 敢；竟敢 |

【同義詞】

brave, meet, face, sustain

| **dash** | v. | 猛撞；猛砸；擊碎 |

【同義詞】

hurry, rush, dart

| **daylight** | n. | 日光；白晝 |

【同義詞】

light, sun, daylight hours

| **deadline** | n. | 截止期限，最後限期 |

【同義詞】

time limit

| **decade** | n. | 十；十年 |

【同義詞】

X, ten

| **decision** | n. | 決定，決心；判斷；結論 |

【同義詞】

settlement, resolution, determination, ruling

declare   n.   宣佈，宣告；聲明

【同義詞】

state, assert, announce, affirm

decoration   n.   裝飾，裝潢

【同義詞】

adornment, ornamentation, embellishment, garnishment

defeat   v.   戰勝，擊敗

【同義詞】

overcome, win, triumph, surpass

defend   v.   防禦；保衛；保護

【同義詞】

protect, safeguard, shield, support

definitely   adv.   明確地；明顯地，清楚地

【同義詞】

absolutely, assuredly, certainly, decidedly

delete   v.   刪除；劃掉（文字等）；擦去

【同義詞】

cancel, remove

delicate   a.   脆的，易碎的；嬌貴的

【同義詞】

mild, soft, fine, exquisite

delight v. 欣喜，愉快

【同義詞】

gratify, gladden, please, cheer

Track**36**

delivery n. 投遞，傳送

【同義詞】

transferal, transference, transmission, dispatch

demand v. 要求，請求

【同義詞】

ask, inquire, require

demonstration n. 證明，示範

【同義詞】

demo, display, evidence, illustration, proof, show

dense a. 密集的，稠密的

【同義詞】

crowded, packed, compact, thick

depart v. 起程，出發；離開，離去

【同義詞】

leave, exit, withdraw, go away

dependable a. 可靠的；可信任的

【同義詞】

trustworthy, honest, honorable

depression n. 沮喪，意氣消沈；不景氣，蕭條（期）

Track**37**

【同義詞】

despair, gloom, melancholy, pessimism, recession, sadness

description n. 描寫；敘述；形容

【同義詞】

portrayal, category, illustrative, depiction

deserve v. 應受，該得

【同義詞】

be worth, be worthy, earn, justify, merit, rate, warrant

designer n. 設計者；構思者；時裝設計師

【同義詞】

creator, inventor, deviser, artificer

desperate a. 情急拼命的，鋌而走險的

【同義詞】

frantic, wild, reckless, rash

destroy v. 毀壞，破壞

【同義詞】

abolish, demolish, eradicate, overthrow, overturn

detail n. 細節；詳情；瑣事；枝節

【同義詞】

element, feature, item, specification

detective n. 偵探；私家偵探

【同義詞】

investigator, private investigator, private eye

detergent n. 洗潔劑，洗衣粉

Track 37

【同義詞】

cleaner, cleanser

determination n. 堅定；果斷，決斷力

【同義詞】

decision, solution

development n. 生長；進化；發展；發達

【同義詞】

growth, evolution, expansion, enlargement

device n. 設備，儀器，裝置

【同義詞】

machine, apparatus, tool, instrument

dialect n. 方言，土話

【同義詞】

speech, idiom, localism, provincialism

dialog n. 對話；交談

【同義詞】

conversation, talk, speech, words

dictation n. 口述；聽寫

【同義詞】

command, charge, order, injunction

中級 Reading & Writing
新制全民英檢
GEPT
The General English Proficiency Test [Intermediate]
NEW
閱讀&寫作 模擬試題 +解答

digest　　v.　消化（食物）

【同義詞】

absorb, ingest, understand, comprehend

diploma　　n.　畢業文憑，學位證書

【同義詞】

degree, academic title, certificate

dirt　　n.　污物；爛泥；灰塵

【同義詞】

filth, grime, smudge

Track **38**

disagree　　v.　不一致，不符

【同義詞】

differ, quarrel, conflict, dispute

disappointment　　n.　失望；掃興，沮喪

【同義詞】

nonfulfillment, nonsuccess, failure, thwarting

disco　　n.　小舞廳；迪斯科舞廳

【同義詞】

discotheque, disco music

discovery　　n.　發現

【同義詞】

detection, unearthing, uncovering

disease　　n.　病，疾病

【同義詞】

sickness, illness, ailment, malady

disgust　　　n.　作嘔

Track**38**

【同義詞】

sicken, offend, repel, revolt

dislike　　　v.　不喜愛，厭惡

【同義詞】

mislike, disrelish, disfavour, object to

distant　　　n.　遠的；久遠的；遠離的

【同義詞】

remote, afar, abroad, out-of-the-way

district　　　n.　區，轄區，行政區

【同義詞】

region, area, zone, territory

divorce　　　v.　離婚

【同義詞】

separate, disjoin, divide, disconnect

donate　　　v.　捐獻，捐贈

【同義詞】

give, contribute, present, bestow

dormitory　　　n.　大寢室，團體寢室

【同義詞】

dorm, student residence

doubtful   a.   懷疑的；疑惑的

【同義詞】

uncertain, unsure, dubious, unbelieving

drag   v.   拉，拖

【同義詞】

pull, draw, haul, tow

dramatic   a.   戲劇的；劇本的

【同義詞】

theatrical, theatric

drawing   n.   描繪，素描；製圖

【同義詞】

sketch, tracing, design, representation

drift   v.   漂，漂流

【同義詞】

float, wander, roam, stray

drown   v.   淹沒，浸濕

【同義詞】

submerge, sink, immerse, inundate

drunk   a.   喝醉的

【同義詞】

intoxicated, tipsy, dizzy

| due | a. | 應支付的；欠款的 |

【同義詞】

indebted, owed, payable, unpaid

| dump | v. | 傾倒；拋棄 |

【同義詞】

empty, unload, discharge, discard

| dynamic | a. | 力的；動力的 |

【同義詞】

active, energetic, forceful, strong

| eager | a. | 熱心的，熱切的 |

【同義詞】

wanting, wishing, desirous, anxious

| earn | v. | 賺得，掙得 |

【同義詞】

get, gain, obtain, make

| earnest | a. | 認真的，誠摯的；重要的，嚴肅的 |

【同義詞】

determined, sincere, serious, devoted

| earthquake | n. | 地震 |

【同義詞】

seism, seismism, microseism, shock

| ease | v. | 減輕，緩和 |

【同義詞】

relieve, reduce, soothe, allay

| economy | n. | 節約，節省 |

【同義詞】

thrift, frugality, saving

| edit | v. | 編輯；校訂 |

【同義詞】

correct, check, rewrite, revise

| education | n. | 教育；培養；訓練 |

【同義詞】

teaching, instruction, tuition, nurture

| efficient | a. | 效率高的；有能力的，能勝任的 |

【同義詞】

efficacious, effectual, effective, valid

| elbow | n. | 肘部 |

【同義詞】

bend, right angle, jostle, hustle

| elderly | n. | 年長的；上了年紀的 |

【同義詞】

Track**40**

old, rather old, oldish, venerable

elect　　　　　v.　選舉；推選

Track**40**

【同義詞】

choose, pick, select, appoint

elegant　　　a.　雅緻的，優美的，漂亮的

【同義詞】

graceful, polished, refined

elemental　　　a.　自然力的；基本的，原始的

【同義詞】

elementary, essential, fundamental, vital

elevator　　　n.　電梯；升降機

【同義詞】

escalator, moving stairs, lift

emergence　　　n.　出現；浮現；露頭

【同義詞】

issue, issuance, outpouring, efflux

emotional　　　a.　感情的

【同義詞】

emotive, affective, sensitive, sentient

employment　　　n.　雇用；受雇

【同義詞】

work, job, service, position

encouragement n. 鼓勵；獎勵；促進

【同義詞】

cheer, promotion, support

engineer n. 工程師

【同義詞】

technician, technologist

entertainment n. 招待，款待

【同義詞】

amusement, diversion, distraction

evidence n. 證據；證詞；證人；物證

【同義詞】

facts, proof, grounds, data

exaggeration n. 誇張，誇大

【同義詞】

overstatement, magnification, puffery, amplification

examination n. 檢查，調查

【同義詞】

scrutiny, scrutinization, inspection

Track**41**

excellence n. 優秀；傑出；卓越

【同義詞】

brilliance, distinction, greatness

exchange v. 交換；調換；兌換

【同義詞】

change, interchange, substitute, switch

expression　　　　n.　表達；表示

Track**41**

【同義詞】

verbalization, pronouncement, communication, informing

extreme　　　a.　末端的，盡頭的

【同義詞】

extravagant, excessive, exaggerated, overdone

facility　　　n.　能力；技能

【同義詞】

edifice, building, structure, plant

fade　　　　v.　褪色，消退；凋謝

【同義詞】

dim, pale, dull, disappear

fail　　　v.　不及格；失敗

【同義詞】

fall, flunk, be unsuccessful

faint　　　v.　頭暈的，行將昏厥的

【同義詞】

中級
Reading & Writing
新制全民英檢
NEW
GEPT
The General English Proficiency Test [Intermediate]
閱讀&寫作 模擬試題+解答

swoon, weaken, black out

fake	n.	偽造；捏造；冒充者，騙子

【同義詞】

imitation, counterfeit

fame	n.	聲譽，名望

【同義詞】

reputation, name, renown, glory

familiar	a.	世所周知的；熟悉的；常見的；普通的

【同義詞】

popular, well-known, friendly, close

fare	v.	吃，進食；過活；遭遇；進展

【同義詞】

eat, be fed, prosper, progress

Track **42**

farewell	n.	再會！告別

【同義詞】

cheerio, good-by, good day, so long

fascinate	v.	迷住，使神魂顛倒；強烈地吸引

【同義詞】

interest, excite, attract, enthrall

feast	n.	盛宴，筵席

【同義詞】

enjoy, like, love, appreciate

feedback　　n.　回饋，反映

【同義詞】

answer, reaction, reply, response

Track**42**

fiction　　n.　小說

【同義詞】

fantasy, untruth, invention, legend

flexible　　a. 可彎曲的，易彎曲的；柔韌的；有彈性的

【同義詞】

pliable, pliant, flexile, tractile

fluent　　a.　流利的，流暢的

【同義詞】

eloquent, articulate, glib, slick

folk　　n.　（某一民族或社會階層中的）廣大成員 . . .

【同義詞】

people, persons, society, public

fortunate　　a.　幸運的，僥倖的

【同義詞】

lucky, auspicious, providential

fortune　　n.　財產，財富；巨款

【同義詞】

riches, wealth, prosperity, treasure

fountain　　n.　泉水；噴泉；水源

【同義詞】

spring, spout, spray, source

| **freeze** | v. | 結冰，凝固 |

【同義詞】

chill, refrigerate, stiffen

| **frequent** | a. | 時常發生的，頻繁的；屢次的 |

【同義詞】

common, constant, recurrent, regular, repeated

Track**43**

| **gang** | n. | （歹徒等的）一幫，一群 |

【同義詞】

group, crew, ring, band

| **glance** | n. | 一瞥；掃視 |

【同義詞】

look, glimpse, skim

| **global** | a. | 球狀的 |

【同義詞】

world-wide, universal, extensive, broad

| **gossip** | n. | 閒話，聊天；流言蜚語 |

【同義詞】

chat, talk, prattle, tattle

grab　　　　　v.　攫取，抓取

Track**43**

【同義詞】

snatch, seize, grasp, grip

grocery　　　n.　食品雜貨店

【同義詞】

market

guarantee　　　v.　保證，擔保

【同義詞】

promise, secure, pledge, swear

H

handicap　　　n.　障礙，不利條件

【同義詞】

hindrance, burden, disadvantage, load

handy　　　a.　手邊的；近便的

【同義詞】

useful, convenient, nearby, available

harm　　　n.　損傷，傷害；危害

【同義詞】

damage, injury, loss

| hint | v. | 暗示 |

【同義詞】

suggest, imply, allude

| horror | n. | 恐怖，震驚 |

【同義詞】

fear, abhorrence, terror, dread

| household | n. | 一家人；家眷；家庭，戶 |

【同義詞】

family, brood, folks

I

Track**44**

| ideal | a. | 理想的，完美的 |

【同義詞】

perfect, faultless, flawless, model

| illegal | a. | 不合法的，非法的；違反規則的 |

【同義詞】

unlawful, criminal, illegitimate

| imagination | n. | 想像力；創造力 |

【同義詞】

dream, fancy, fantasy

| imitate | v. | 模仿 |

【同義詞】

follow, trace, copy, duplicate

| **immediate** | a. | 立即的，即刻的 |

Track44

【同義詞】

direct, instant, prompt, urgent

| **imply** | v. | 暗指；暗示；意味著 |

【同義詞】

suggest, hint, infer

| **impress** | v. | 給...極深的印象；使感動 |

【同義詞】

affect, strike, fix, establish

| **incident** | n. | 事件；事變 |

【同義詞】

happening, event, occurrence, adventure

| **independence** | n. | 獨立；自主；自立 |

【同義詞】

autonomy, freedom, liberty, self-reliance, sovereignty

| **influence** | v. | 影響，作用 |

【同義詞】

sway, affect, move, induce

| **informal** | a. | 非正式的，非正規的 |

【同義詞】

casual, cozy, easy, familiar, relaxed

ingredient n. （混合物的）組成部分；（烹調的）原料

【同義詞】

component, element, factor, item, part

injure v. 傷害；損害；毀壞

【同義詞】

damage, harm, hurt, wound

input n. 投入；輸入

【同義詞】

stimulant, stimulation, stimulus

insert v. 插入；嵌入

【同義詞】

introduce, inject, enter, put in

Track**45**

instead adv. 作為，替代

【同義詞】

in place of, rather than

instruction n. 教學，講授；教育

【同義詞】

advice, education, guidance, lecture, lesson

insult n. 侮辱，羞辱

【同義詞】

abuse, dishonor, offense

intermediate a. 中間的，居中的；中型的

【同義詞】

middle, intervening, in between

Track**45**

interpret v. 解釋，說明，詮釋

【同義詞】

explain, clarify, translate, analyze

interrupt v. 打斷，中斷

【同義詞】

discontinue, disrupt, disturb, intrude, pause

invention n. 發明，創造

【同義詞】

creation, design, device

J

jealous a. 妒忌的

【同義詞】

envious, covetous, desirous of

journey n. 旅行

【同義詞】

trip, voyage, tour, expedition

joyful a. 高興的，充滿喜悅的；使人高興的

【同義詞】

glad, happy, cheerful, blissful

junior	a.	年紀較輕的

【同義詞】

younger, lower, lesser, secondary

junk	n.	廢棄的舊物

【同義詞】

rubbish, trash, scrap, litter

justice	n.	正義；公平；正當的理由；合法

【同義詞】

fairness, fair play, impartiality, fair-mindedness

Track46

keen	a.	熱心的，熱衷的，深切的

【同義詞】

sharp, cutting, fine, acute

keyboard	n.	鍵盤

【同義詞】

keypad

kidnap	v.	誘拐

【同義詞】

snatch, abduct, carry off

| **kindness** | n. | 仁慈；和藹；好意 |

Track**46**

【同義詞】

goodness, benevolence

| **kneel** | v. | 跪下 |

【同義詞】

bow, kowtow

L

| **label** | n. | 貼紙；標籤；商標 |

【同義詞】

name, brand, title, tag

| **labor** | n. | 勞動 |

【同義詞】

work, employment, job, occupation

| **lack** | v. | 不足，缺乏 |

【同義詞】

need, want

| **landlady** | n. | 女房東；女主人 |

【同義詞】

proprietress, mistress

中級 Reading & Writing

新制全民英檢

GEPT

The General English Proficiency Test [Intermediate]

NEW

閱讀&寫作 模擬試題 +解答

landlord　　n.　房東；主人

【同義詞】

owner, landowner, landholder, property-owner, proprietor

landmark　　n.　地標，陸標

【同義詞】

turning-point, milestone

landscape　　n.　風景，景色

【同義詞】

scene, aspect, outlook, prospect

laughter　　n.　笑；笑聲

【同義詞】

laugh, giggle, snicker

Track**47**

launch　　v.　使（船）下水；發射；發動，展開

【同義詞】

start, introduce, spring, set afloat

laundry　　n.　洗衣店；送洗的衣服

【同義詞】

wash, washing, dirty clothes

lawn　　n.　草坪，草地

【同義詞】

greensward, grassplot, grass, turf

leaflet　　n.　傳單；單張印刷品

【同義詞】

handbill, bill, brochure, pamphlet

leak   v.   漏洞，裂縫

Track**47**

【同義詞】

drip, dribble, run out

leap   v.   跳，跳躍

【同義詞】

jump, spring, vault, hop

lecture   n.   授課；演講

【同義詞】

speech, talk, sermon, address

legend   n.   傳說；傳奇故事；傳奇文學

【同義詞】

story, fiction, myth, fable

leisure   n.   閒暇，空暇時間

【同義詞】

free time, spare time, rest, repose

liar   n.   說謊的人

【同義詞】

fibber, falsifier, fabricator, perjurer

liberty   n.   自由；自由權

【同義詞】

中級 Reading & Writing
新制全民英檢
GEPT
The General English Proficiency Test [Intermediate]
NEW
閱讀&寫作 模擬試題 +解答

freedom, independence, autonomy, emancipation

librarian	n.	圖書館館長；圖書館員

【同義詞】

bibliothec, person in charge of a library

license	n.	許可，特許

【同義詞】

permission, allowance, consent

lifetime	n.	一生，終身

【同義詞】

life, lifespan

lighten	v.	變亮；發亮

【同義詞】

brighten, cheer, clear, illuminate, shine

limit	n.	界線；界限

【同義詞】

border, boundary, brink, limitation

Track**48**

lively	a.	精力充沛的；活潑的，輕快的

【同義詞】

exciting, bright, cheerful, vivid

load	n.	負載；負荷；憂慮

【同義詞】

burden, pressure, weight

loan　　　　n.　借出；借出的東西

【同義詞】

advance, give

Track**48**

lobby　　　　n.　大廳；門廊

【同義詞】

entrance, passageway, foyer

location　　n.　位置；場所，所在地

【同義詞】

site, spot, point, locality

logical　　a.　邏輯學的

【同義詞】

reasonable, sensible, sound, sane

loneliness　n.　孤獨，寂寞

【同義詞】

aloneness, desolation, isolation, lonesomeness

loose　　　a.　鬆的，寬的；鬆散的

【同義詞】

limp, drooping, unfastened, untied

lousy　　　a.　盡是蝨子的；不潔的

【同義詞】

dirty, filthy, miserable, rotten, stinky

loyal　　　a.　忠誠的，忠心的

中級 Reading & Writing
新制全民英檢
GEPT
The General English Proficiency Test [Intermediate]
NEW

閱讀&寫作 模擬試題 +解答

【同義詞】

trustworthy, devoted, faithful, constant

| **luxury** | n. | 奢侈，奢華 |

【同義詞】

luxuriousness, luxe, sumptuousness, lavishness

Track**49**

M

| **magical** | a. | 魔術的，魔法的 |

【同義詞】

charming, enchanting, witching

| **magnificent** | a. | 壯麗的，宏偉的，宏大的 |

【同義詞】

splendid, grand, stately, majestic

| **maintain** | v. | 保持，主張 |

【同義詞】

keep, uphold, possess, support

| **major** | a. | 較大的；主要的 |

【同義詞】

larger, greater, superior, higher

| **management** | n. | 管理；經營；處理 |

【同義詞】

administration, leadership, supervision

mature　　　　a.　成熟的，熟練的

【同義詞】

ripe, developed, mellow, fit, ready

Track**49**

mess　　　　　v.　弄髒，弄亂；弄糟，毀壞

【同義詞】

dirty, disfigure, contaminate, pollute

method　　　　n.　方法，辦法

【同義詞】

system, way, manner, means, procedure

mild　　　　　a.　溫和的，溫柔的

【同義詞】

gentle, kind, calm, warm

misunderstand　　　v.　誤會；曲解

【同義詞】

misapprehend, misread, misconstrue, misconceive

modest　　　a.　謙虛的，審慎的

【同義詞】

humble, bashful, shy, quiet

mood　　　n.　心情，心境，情緒

【同義詞】

feeling, temperament, humor, disposition

N

native　　　a.　天生的；本土的，本國的

【同義詞】

natural, original, indigenous

nearby　　　a.　附近的

【同義詞】

around, close, near, neighboring

neat　　　　a.　整潔的；整齊的

【同義詞】

clean, orderly, trim, tidy

neglect　　v.　忽視，忽略

【同義詞】

overlook, disregard, ignore

neighborhood　　n.　鄰近地區

【同義詞】

district, region, surroundings

newcomer　　n.　新來的人；新近到達的移民

【同義詞】

beginner, greenhorn, novice, starter

nightmare　　n.　夢魘；惡夢

【同義詞】

ordeal, trial

O

obvious a. 明顯的；顯著的

【同義詞】

understandable, apparent, clear, plain

occasion n. 場合，時刻；重大活動，盛典

【同義詞】

time, instance, case, spot

option n. 選擇；選擇權；選擇自由

【同義詞】

choice, alternative, substitute, equivalent

oral a. 口頭的，口述的

【同義詞】

spoken, voiced, vocalized, sounded

origin n. 起源；由來；起因

【同義詞】

beginning, start, infancy, birth

outcome n. 結果；結局；後果

【同義詞】

result, consequence, effect, upshot

output n. 出產；生產

【同義詞】

turnout, production

Track**51**

| **outstanding** | a. | 顯著的；傑出的；重要的 |

【同義詞】

important, great, famous

| **overcome** | v. | 戰勝；克服 |

【同義詞】

conquer, defeat, upset, overpower

| **overlook** | v. | 看漏；忽略 |

【同義詞】

neglect, ignore, disregard, skip

| **overthrow** | v. | 推翻，打倒；廢除 |

【同義詞】

upset, demolish, crush, beat, overpower

P

| **pace** | n. | 速度；進度 |

【同義詞】

rate, speed, stride, walk

| **parade** | n. | 行進，行列，遊行 |

【同義詞】

show, display, review

| **paradise** | n. | 樂園，極樂 |

【同義詞】

heaven, bliss, glory, ecstasy

participate v. 參加，參與

Track**51**

【同義詞】

partake, take part in, have a hand in, enter into

particularly adv. 特別，尤其

【同義詞】

chiefly, especially, specially

partnership n. 合夥或合作關係

【同義詞】

alliance, association, union

passion n. 熱情，激情

【同義詞】

emotion, enthusiasm, craze, fervor

pat v. 輕拍，輕打

Track**52**

【同義詞】

tap, stroke, rap

penalty n. 處罰；刑罰

【同義詞】

punishment, penalty, sentence, condemnation

permission n. 允許，許可，同意

【同義詞】

中級 Reading & Writing
新制全民英檢
GEPT
The General English Proficiency Test [Intermediate]

NEW

閱讀&寫作 模擬試題 +解答

Track**52**

leave, consent, license

personality　　　　n.　人格，品格

【同義詞】

identity, individuality

pity　　　　　n.　憐憫；同情

【同義詞】

sympathy, sorrow, compassion, mercy

possibly　　adv.　也許，可能

【同義詞】

perhaps, maybe

postpone　　v.　使延期，延遲，延緩

【同義詞】

delay, defer, suspend

present　　a.　出席的，在場的

【同義詞】

actual, contemporary, current

previous　　a.　先的，前的，以前的

【同義詞】

prior, earlier, former, preceding

probably　　adv.　大概，或許，很可能

【同義詞】

likely, presumably, supposedly

promotion   n.   提升，晉級

【同義詞】

advancement, improvement, lift, rise

property   n.   財產，資產；所有物

【同義詞】

possession, holdings, belongings

Track 53

qualification   n.   資格；能力

【同義詞】

competence, competency, fitness, satisfactoriness

quantity   n.   量

【同義詞】

amount, number, sum, measure

quarrel   v.   爭吵；不和；吵鬧

【同義詞】

argument, disagreement, fuss

quote   v.   引用；引述

【同義詞】

cite, illustrate, repeat

中級 Reading & Writing
新制全民英檢
GEPT
The General English Proficiency Test [Intermediate]
NEW
閱讀&寫作 模擬試題 +解答

Track **53**

recognition　　　n.　認出，識別；認識

【同義詞】

identification, recollection, remembrance, recall

recovery　　n.　重獲；復得

【同義詞】

recapturing, retaking, retrieval

recreation　　　n.　消遣；娛樂，遊戲

【同義詞】

play, amusement, entertainment, pleasure

reduce　　　v.　減少；縮小；降低

【同義詞】

lessen, lower, decrease, diminish

reflect　　　v.　反射；照出，映出

【同義詞】

mirror, send back

refresh　　　v.　使清新，使清涼

【同義詞】

renew, revive, reanimate, regenerate

refuse　　　v.　拒絕；拒受；不准

【同義詞】

decline, reject

relax   v.   使鬆弛，使鬆懈，放鬆

Track**54**

【同義詞】

rest, loosen, ease up

rely   v.   依靠，依賴；依仗

【同義詞】

trust, confide, depend on, count on

replace   v.   把 . . . 放回；取代

【同義詞】

succeed, supply, come after, substitute for

represent   v.   描繪；表示

【同義詞】

portray, depict, illustrate, symbolize

request   v.   要求，請求

【同義詞】

apply, require

requirement   n.   需要；必需品

【同義詞】

need, necessity, urgent need, must

rescue   v.   援救；營救；挽救

【同義詞】

release, retrieve, salvage, redeem

Track**54**

responsibility　　n.　責任

【同義詞】

duty, obligation, office

S

scare　　v.　驚嚇，使恐懼

【同義詞】

frighten, alarm, startle, unnerve

schedule　　n.　表；清單；目錄

【同義詞】

list, index, post, slate

selection　　n.　選擇；選拔

【同義詞】

choosing, picking, hand-picking, singling out

significance　　n.　重要性，重要

【同義詞】

meaning, connotation, implication

sociable　　a.　好交際的；善交際的

【同義詞】

friendly, congenial, amiable, cordial

sorrow　　n.　悲痛，悲哀，悲傷，憂傷

【同義詞】

grief, sadness, regret, trouble

spiritual　　a.　精神的，心靈的

【同義詞】

religious, sacred, holy

splendid　　a.　有光彩的；燦爛的

【同義詞】

gorgeous, glorious, wonderful, magnificent

staff　　　　n.　全體職員，全體工作人員

【同義詞】

group, committee, personnel, crew

steady　　a.　穩固的，平穩的

【同義詞】

constant, fixed, inert, regular

strategy　　n.　戰略；戰略學

【同義詞】

planning, management, tactics, manipulation

strength　　n.　力量，力氣；實力；效力

【同義詞】

power, energy, force, vigor

suitable　　a.　適當的；合適的；適宜的

【同義詞】

fitting, proper, timely, favorable

| **suppose** | v. | 猜想，以為 |

Track**55**

【同義詞】

believe, think, imagine, consider

| **surely** | adv. | 確實，無疑，一定 |

【同義詞】

firmly, confidently, unhesitatingly

T

| **tasty** | a. | 美味的；高雅的，大方的 |

【同義詞】

good-tasting, savory

| **temporary** | a. | 臨時的；暫時的，一時的 |

【同義詞】

passing, momentary, transient, short-lived

| **tend** | v. | 照管，照料；護理；管理 |

【同義詞】

attend, administer, help, mind

| **tendency** | n. | 傾向；癖性；天分 |

【同義詞】

inclination, leaning, bent

tender　　　a.　嫩的；柔軟的

【同義詞】

soft, delicate, gentle, kind

thankful　　　a.　感謝的，感激的；欣慰的

【同義詞】

indebted, grateful, appreciative, obliged

thorough　　　a.　徹底的；完全的

【同義詞】

complete, intensive, full, sweeping

Track**56**

thoughtful　　　a.　深思的，沈思的

【同義詞】

kind, considerate, sympathetic, concerned

timid　　　a.　膽小的，易受驚的

【同義詞】

shy, bashful, meek

transfer　　v.　搬；轉換；調動

【同義詞】

deliver, pass, hand over, sign over

transform　　v.　使改變；使改觀；將 ... 改成

【同義詞】

change, convert, alter

typical　　　a.　典型的，有代表性的

Track56

【同義詞】

representative, symbolic, characteristic, distinctive

U

| **understanding** | n. | 了解；理解；領會；認識 |

【同義詞】

comprehension, cognition, consciousness

| **undertake** | v. | 試圖；著手做；進行，從事 |

【同義詞】

try, attempt, endeavor

| **upset** | v. | 弄翻，打翻；傾覆 |

【同義詞】

overturn, unsettle, capsize, tip over

| **urge** | v. | 催促；力勸；激勵；慫恿 |

【同義詞】

push, force, drive, plead

| **urgent** | a. | 緊急的，急迫的 |

【同義詞】

pressing, important, imperative, compelling

| **usage** | n. | 使用，用法；處理 |

【同義詞】

method, practice, way, use

 V

Track **57**

vacant　　　a.　空的；空白的

【同義詞】

unoccupied, empty, void, blank

vague　　　a.　模糊不清的，朦朧的

【同義詞】

unclear, indistinct, indefinite

vain　　　　a.　愛虛榮的，自負的，炫耀的

【同義詞】

unsuccessful, ineffectual, futile, fruitless

valid　　　　a.　合法的；有效的；妥當的

【同義詞】

legal, effective, just

valuable　　a.　值錢的，貴重的

【同義詞】

costly, expensive, high-priced

vanish　　　v.　突然不見；消失

【同義詞】

disappear, fade, perish, go away

中級
Reading & Writing
新制全民英檢
GEPT
The General English Proficiency Test [Intermediate]
NEW

閱讀&寫作 模擬試題+解答

Track **57**

vary	v.	使不同；變更；修改

【同義詞】

change, differ, alter, deviate

vast	a.	廣闊的，浩瀚的，廣大的

【同義詞】

large, immense, great, enormous

verbal	a.	言辭上的；言語的，字句的

【同義詞】

oral, spoken, said

violate	v.	違犯；違背，違反

【同義詞】

break, trespass, infringe

vital	a.	生命的；維持生命所必需的

【同義詞】

necessary, important, essential, fundamental

vivid	a.	鮮豔的；鮮明的

【同義詞】

bright, brilliant, strong, clear

voluntary	a.	自願的，志願的

【同義詞】

intentional, intended

voyage	n.	航海，航行，乘船旅遊

【同義詞】

journey, migration, passage, tour, travel, trip

W

Track **58**

| **wage** | n. | 薪水；報酬 |

【同義詞】

pay, payment, salary

| **warmth** | n. | 溫暖 |

【同義詞】

fervidity, vehemence, zeal

| **warn** | v. | 警告；告誡；提醒 |

【同義詞】

inform, notify, caution

| **wealthy** | a. | 富的；富裕的；豐富的 |

【同義詞】

rich, affluent, prosperous, moneyed

| **withdraw** | v. | 抽回；拉開；移開 |

【同義詞】

retreat, recede, retire, quit

| **worthwhile** | a. | 值得做的 |

【同義詞】

meaningful, useful, valuable, worthy

wrestle	v.	摔角

【同義詞】

struggle, battle, fight

yard	n.	院子；天井；庭院

【同義詞】

court, courtyard, inner court, quadrangle

year	n.	年，一年

【同義詞】

session, period, space, term

yearn	v.	渴望；嚮往

【同義詞】

desire, crave, long for, wish for

yell	v.	叫喊；吼叫聲

【同義詞】

call, cry, bawl, exclaim

yield	v.	生產；產生

【同義詞】

produce, give, grant, bear

yoke　　　n.　軛，牛軛

【同義詞】

harness, shackle, bridle

youngster　　　n.　小孩

【同義詞】

child, minor, youth, kid

Z

Track**59**

zealous　　　a.　熱心的；狂熱的

【同義詞】

enthusiastic, fervent, earnest, ardent

zero　　　n.　零；零號

【同義詞】

nothing, naught, nil, none

zip　　n.　子彈等飛射聲，撕布聲；活力，精力

【同義詞】

vigor, energy, vitality

zone　　　n.　地帶；地區

【同義詞】

region, area, territory, place

國家圖書館出版品預行編目資料

NEW GEPT新制全民英檢(中級)：閱讀&寫作模擬試題+解答/
張文娟著. -- 初版. -- 新北市 ： 雅典文化事業有限公司,
民111.12　面 ；　公分. -- (英語工具書 ； 19)
ISBN 978-626-96423-4-2(平裝)
1.CST: 英語 2.CST: 能力測驗
805.1892　　　　　　　　　　111015438

英語工具書系列　　19

NEW GEPT新制全民英檢(中級)：閱讀&寫作模擬試題+解答

作者／張文娟
責編／張文娟
美術編輯／姚恩涵
封面設計／林鈺恆

法律顧問：方圓法律事務所／涂成樞律師

總經銷：永續圖書有限公司

永續圖書線上購物網
www.foreverbooks.com.tw

雲端回函卡

出版日／2022年12月

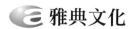
雅典文化

出
版
社
　22103　　新北市汐止區大同路三段194號9樓之1
TEL　　(02) 8647-3663
FAX　　(02) 8647-3660